Dragon Blood 1: Pliethin

Dragon Blood 1
Pliethin

Avril Sabine

Cracked Acorn Productions
Australia

Dragon Blood 1: Pliethin

Published by

Cracked Acorn Productions

PO Box 1365

Gympie, Queensland 4570

Australia

978-1-925131-20-8 (Kindle)

978-1-925617-62-7 (EPUB)

978-1-925131-34-5 (Print)

Genre: Young Adult Urban Fantasy

Cover design by Caitlyn Petersen

For my kids. I could list a million reasons why, but there is one reason that sums up the majority of them. For being yourselves.

Sixteen-year-old Amber's life, that was once completely normal, is dramatically changed when she is forced to move to a small Queensland town west of Brisbane. Suddenly dragons are no longer creatures of myth. Amber becomes caught up in their world of clans, survival of the fittest, ancient traditions, dangerous enemies and dragon warriors.

*

This story was written by an Australian author using Australian spelling.

Name and Place Pronunciation

Like many names there is more than one way to pronounce the following ones. These are the pronunciations used in this series.

Names:

Alsandair (ahl–san–dare)

Anrai (arn–ree)

Bredon (bread–en)

Chait (single syllable, rhymes with hate)

Daray (dah–ray)

Doneele (donny–lee)

Emlyn (em–lin)

Gair (rhymes with hair)

Gethin (geh-thin)

Isleen (ish-lean)

Kiani (key-ah-knee)

Laren (lah-rin)

Maira (may-rah)

Orin (oh-rin)

Paili (pah-lee)

Queran (qwhere-rin)

Rhobert (row-bert)

Rian (ree-in)

Ronan (row-nen)

Tahmid (tar-mid)

Turi (two-ree)

Other pronunciations:

Erilan (era-len)

Feralenzi (fair-a-len-zee)

Pliethin (plea-thin)

Temolae (tem-oh-lay)

Chapter One

Amber swirled the dishcloth through the water in the kitchen sink and watched as the suds parted. Her chestnut hair fell in waves around her shoulders and her brown eyes remained focused on the water. There had to be a way to convince her mother to change her mind. "I don't see why we had to move to Hicksville. How am I meant to see my friends? It's nearly four hours to the city." Amber looked over her shoulder at her mother. She still couldn't believe her mother had made her leave Brisbane partway through year twelve.

Donna grabbed the salt and pepper shakers from the middle of the kitchen table, putting them in the pantry. She had short blond hair and blue eyes that narrowed as she faced Amber. "Stop calling it Hicksville. It upsets your grandmother when you do that."

"Yeah, well it upsets me being here."

"Don't start. Just do the dishes."

"We shouldn't have had to come here. Once you move a few hours away from the Australian coast you might as well be in the desert, at least as far as civilisation is concerned. Grandma could have stayed with us. She would have been able to survive the city for six weeks. Why should I be punished because she broke her arm?"

"Amber."

She ignored the warning tone in her mother's voice, determined to convince her. "I could have stayed behind with Dad. Jay got to."

"Jasper's at uni."

"And I don't see why I have to go to school here. My school could have given me whatever work we'd cover this term. How do you expect me to pass school and get into uni next year if you're going to make me change schools like this?"

"Dishes! Now!"

Amber muttered under her breath as she turned back to the sink and swept the cutlery off the bench and into the water. She plunged her hand into the sink then yelped. "I cut myself. I don't see why Grandma can't have a dishwasher." Nothing had gone right since her mother had forced her to move here. She fought against the anger and frustration that made her want to scream.

"Amber!"

She muttered loud enough for her mother to hear. "Stupid town. Stupid school. Stupid house." She put the last of the cutlery in the draining rack and pulled the plug. Drying her hands on the rear of her jeans, she turned to face her mother. "I want to stay with Dad. You're the one who wanted to come here. I want to stay at home. You don't need me. It doesn't take two people to look after an old woman with a broken arm." Why wouldn't her mother listen to her? If only she could figure out how to make her listen.

Donna opened her mouth to reply when the kitchen door opened and Helen stepped in. She had her arm in plaster and a sling, wore wire-rimmed glasses, was bony rather than slim and had grey hair. She glanced between Amber and Donna until her gaze came to a rest on Amber. "You're not still complaining about being here, are you? Never known a kid who could whinge so much."

Amber glared at Helen. "It's probably hereditary."

"That's it. To your room. Now! I won't have you talking to your grandmother like that." Donna pointed towards the kitchen door.

Amber turned her glare on her mother. She had

not started that. Her grandmother had. "Might as well sit in my room the whole time we're here. Nothing else to do. All my friends are back home. So even if there was something to do, I've got no one to do it with." She pushed the door open and stepped into the hallway, the door closing behind her. She stomped up the stairs, her anger carrying her halfway up them before she noticed a droplet of blood had formed on her finger. Sighing, she started back down the stairs to ask where the bandaids were kept. About to push the kitchen door open, she froze as she heard the raised voices. Did she really want to step into another argument between her mother and grandmother?

"Don't take that tone with me, Mum. Amber is having a difficult time here. She's missing her friends. She's not usually like this."

Amber grinned. No, she was sometimes worse. She pressed her ear against the door as their voices lowered.

"You've been here nearly a week and that girl has sulked or carried on the entire time. I kept telling you the way you were raising your kids would turn them into spoilt, inconsiderate brats. And you haven't even told her yet, have you?"

Amber held her breath, waiting to hear what her mother would say. The silence stretched out long enough she began to wonder if they were whispering. The sound of a chair scraping on the floor had Amber tensing as she wondered if her mother was headed towards the door.

"I'm waiting for the right moment."

"You're an idiot, Donna. She'll figure it out eventually. Or is that what you're waiting for?"

"I just know she's going to take it hard."

"That's not an excuse. You were always lacking in backbone. I sometimes wonder if I brought the wrong baby home from the hospital when I had you."

There was another silence and Amber fought the urge to burst into the kitchen to make her grandmother apologise.

"I'll tell her when she's settled into her new school."

Helen snorted. "I'll believe that when I see it. She's not interested in fitting in. And what about the bedrooms? She whined you had the bigger one and you handed it straight over. No backbone. And now you have no ensuite."

"It was unimportant."

That was news to Amber. She hadn't cared about the size of the room, or having an ensuite, she'd just been looking for a way to convince her mother to let her go home.

"I might as well go to bed. I'm wasting my time trying to talk to you, Donna."

Amber scurried away from the kitchen door and up the stairs as quietly as possible. The last thing she needed was for her mother to catch her listening at the door. Even if it had started out as an accident. She closed her bedroom door behind her and leaned against it in relief.

She didn't think Helen knew how to be a grandmother. Her best friend, Crystal, had a grandmother who baked biscuits and cakes and called her 'love'. She was stuck with a grandmother who terrorised small children, glared more than she smiled and always listed people's shortcomings rather than their achievements.

Amber locked the bedroom door and grabbed a tissue to dab at her bleeding finger. She watched the blood stain the tissue before she crossed the bedroom to the French doors and flung them open. Stepping onto the small balcony that wasn't much wider than the doors, she scrunched up the tissue and pushed it into a pocket of her jeans.

Leaning on the balcony rail, she wished she was back in her own room. It had only been six days, but it felt like so much longer. She just wanted to go home. The only benefit of being here was that when she looked at the stars, they seemed closer. If she were into astronomy she'd have been happy to move. But she wasn't. She had a life. One she liked very much. And it wasn't here. She'd lost count of the amount of times she'd told her mother those words. It had made no difference. Nothing had.

Amber stared up at the stars, her mouth dropping open. Silhouetted in moonlight were two large… birds. At least she guessed that's what they were. They were a blur of rapid motion as they attacked each other. She turned to hurry inside and grab her phone to take a picture. A crash against the roof of the house made her spin back. She looked up in time to see a man slide over the edge and land in a heap at her feet.

Amber stumbled backwards into her room, opening her mouth to scream. The man lurched to his feet and lunged for her, covering her mouth with his hand. Meeting his gaze, she recognised him. It was a boy she'd caught staring at her in class today. One she hadn't minded staring back at. Her fear eased slightly, only to increase again as she noticed the blood streaking his left arm. Four long, deep gashes ran down his flesh.

He staggered. His hand left her mouth as he grabbed her shoulders to steady himself, looking like he'd collapse at any second. Amber seized him by the arms and nearly let go as the blood from his wound made the cut on her finger burn. And not just burn. It felt like acid shooting through her finger, quickly becoming a dull ache. Putting her shoulder under his arm, she slid an arm around his waist and helped him further into her room. She paused, unsure what to do next.

Blood dripped onto the polished timber floor and Amber groaned. "Ensuite, before you bleed everywhere."

He breathed shallowly, his jaw clenched. "Lock the doors."

"As soon as you're in the bathroom." This was crazy. He was worried about locking doors and she was concerned about blood on the floor. What she should do was call an ambulance.

He pulled away from her, pressed a hand against his wounds and stumbled across the room to the open door of her ensuite. Amber watched him for a couple of seconds before she turned and locked the French doors, trying not to get blood on them. She hesitated. Should she call for an ambulance or let him know what she was doing first? And what on earth had he been doing on her roof? A sound of falling bottles made her dash to the ensuite.

She stopped in the doorway. The basin tap ran and

blood swirled in the water as it went down the drain. Lotions and bottles lay on their side on the vanity and tiled floor. Her unexpected guest sat with his back against the timber door of the vanity, his eyes closed.

Fear for herself was replaced with fear for the boy. How much blood could a person lose before they died? "I'll call an ambulance."

"No!" His eyes opened to stare at her. They were a golden brown, his brown hair sun streaked with a similar colour.

"You can't expect me to let you bleed to death on my floor." Amber took a step backwards.

He smiled then winced. "You're Amber, aren't you?" At her nod, he said, "You're in my English and Art classes."

She nodded again. "I don't know your name."

"Kade."

She watched the blood drip down his arm, even with the pressure of his hand against the gashes. "You need a doctor."

Kade shook his head. "I only need some help cleaning it up."

They both turned at the firm knock on Amber's bedroom door and Kade tried to struggle to his feet.

Amber knelt beside him to press him back to the floor. "Don't be stupid. You'll fall over." She wasn't sure why she whispered. She should have been calling out that they needed an ambulance.

Kade grabbed her hand. "Don't let them in. Please." He kept his voice as low as hers.

Amber jerked her hand out of his bloody one, ignoring the knock that came again. She stared at the cut on her finger, Kade's blood smeared across her hand. "What the hell have you got in your blood? Acid?"

Kade swore softly, grabbing her hand. He swore again when he peered at the cut. "Wash it. Immediately."

Amber put her hand under the still running tap. Fear slid through her. Did he have some sort of disease? Scenarios ran through her mind. Each worse than the last until she came to an image of her body so diseased it was falling apart. She grabbed the soap and washed her hand harder. "What's wrong with you?"

"You'll live."

Amber looked down at him. "That's not what I asked."

"It's what you're thinking."

"What are you? A mind reader?"

Kade tried to smile. It turned into a grimace after a momentarily successful start. "Your expression."

Before Amber could reply, there was a harder knock at the door. "Amber? Honey? Let me in."

"Don't let her in," Kade whispered urgently. "Please."

She raised her voice. "I'm in the bathroom, Mum."

"I need to talk to you," Donna called through the door.

"Well you can't. I'm not about to sit around having conversations while I'm naked." Amber turned her back on Kade's fleeting grin and waited for her mother's reply.

"Come to my room when you're finished?"

"I suppose." When there was silence on the other side of the door, Amber turned back to Kade, lowering her voice again. "What am I meant to do with you?"

"A bit of pressure on the scratches I can't cover would be good but don't use the hand with the cut."

Amber sat facing him and pressed her hand against his arm, trying not to think about the blood that quickly coated her hand. "I can't sit here all night. My mum will be back looking for me if I take too long." Why wouldn't he let her call an ambulance? Had he been doing something illegal? And how had he got onto her roof?

"Help isn't far away." Kade closed his eyes.

"You're not going to pass out on me, are you?" If he did, she was ringing an ambulance no matter what he said.

Kade opened his eyes. "Would that bother you?"

Amber met his gaze. She should have been the one with eyes that colour. They would have suited her name much better than the plain brown ones she had. But at least she couldn't complain about her hair, which fell in rich chestnut waves around her shoulders.

"Maybe I should be worried about you." Kade raised an eyebrow.

"What?"

"Never mind." He shook his head. "Can you open the balcony doors now?"

"I thought I was supposed to lock them."

"Now I want you to unlock them."

"Don't talk to me like I'm an idiot."

Kade closed his eyes for a second then spoke with exaggerated patience. "Please open the doors. My friends are on the balcony waiting to be let in."

Chapter Two

"What?" Amber leapt to her feet, running over to the glass doors. She stared at the two shadowy figures standing on the balcony. A glance over her shoulder showed Kade still leaned against the vanity. She hesitated as the figures came into the light. Amber recognised them from school. One was in her English class, the other Art. She opened the doors and stepped back so they could enter. This would have to be the most interesting thing that had happened since she'd arrived and she had no idea what to think or do.

"I'm Maira, that's Brann." Maira smiled, chunky silver and black bracelets glinting as she gestured towards her companion. Maira had black hair cut level with her smile, green eyes that glanced around the room and skin a couple of shades darker than Brann's well tanned skin. Brann was easily six foot.

He had curly brown hair longer than Maira's, deep blue eyes and a friendly grin.

"I'm Amber." Questions crowded her mind and she didn't know what to ask first.

"Oh be patient. We're coming," Maira muttered as she strode towards the bathroom.

Amber turned to stare at Kade in confusion. He hadn't spoken a word. She followed Maira into the bathroom. "Ah… have you considered it might be best to call an ambulance?"

"He'll be fine. It's not as bad as it looks." Maira washed out a cloth she took from the leather backpack Brann carried. She bent to wipe at Kade's wound.

"Careful," Kade growled.

"Baby." Maira rose to wash out the cloth.

"That'll teach you for taking off without us." Brann leaned against the door frame of the bathroom, the backpack at his feet.

"Will you lot be much longer in my bathroom? I have to wash. My mum's waiting to talk to me and for some reason Kade doesn't want anyone to know he's here. If I take too long, she might come back." Amber looked at each of them, still not certain what to do. If she told her mother, her grandmother was sure to find out and Helen would think of some way to blame this on her.

"Amber?"

She faced Brann.

"Can't you go and see your mum while we sort Kade out?"

Amber started to answer when a tearing sound made her turn towards Maira and Kade. Maira dropped the sleeveless shirt, she'd torn away from Kade, onto the floor. Amber's gaze searched for scissors. There were none. The dark shirt had looked new and of the same material as Kade's long pants. Amber realised the dull black pants they all wore were made of leather. Maira also wore a body hugging leather vest.

"Are you lot in some sort of gang?"

Kade chuckled. "Do you always do that?"

"What?"

"Brann asked you a question. You ignored it."

Amber turned back to Brann. "What was it again?"

"Doesn't matter. We're nearly finished and then you can have your bathroom back." Brann reached into the backpack to pull out a small first aid kit.

Amber paled when Maira took a fine needle from the box. "You're not going to…" she swallowed hard. She held up a hand to indicate 'stop', then staggered to the toilet to sit on the closed lid. "On second thought, I don't want to know." She leaned forward, eyes closed and breathed through her mouth. Her stomach somersaulted and she pressed her hand against her lips only to realise it was the bloodstained one.

Taking the single step to the shower, she turned it on to wash her hand clean. Next she brought water to her face to clean off the rest of the blood. Turning off the tap she shakily grabbed her towel and covered her face with it. Sitting on the toilet lid, she kept her face buried.

"Are you okay?" Brann asked.

Amber could only shake her head. She was afraid to speak for fear she'd lose her dinner. Blood she could handle, medical procedures involving needles was too much.

"You can look now. I'm finished," Maira said.

Amber took a cautious look. Neat stitches marched along the gashes. Kade's normally golden brown skin was pale and his eyes were closed with his head tilted back. While she watched, Maira touched Kade's forehead and his eyes popped open. Maira nodded her head, gathered up the first aid kit, cleaned up the blood and followed Brann out of the bathroom, the backpack slung over his shoulder.

"Why do I keep feeling like there are conversations I can't hear?" Amber slid her towel over the towel rack where it hung bunched up.

Kade rose carefully to his feet. "Has anyone ever told you what an interesting imagination you have?"

"Has anyone ever told you you're full of it?"

Kade laughed. "Not often." He moved towards the doorway then looked back at her. "I'll see you at school tomorrow."

"What?" She hurried to his side snagging his hand so he couldn't move away. She wanted answers and she wasn't about to let him go before she got them.

"I haven't said thank you, have I?"

"What happened? How did you end up on the roof? What attacked you? How did your friends know to find you here? And what did Maira give you for pain? I don't know any tablets that work that quickly." She was finally able to ask some of the questions that had been swirling around in her mind.

"Full of questions, aren't you?"

"I haven't even started."

Kade tugged his hand out of hers. "Then don't bother. I'm not going to answer them."

"I deserve some sort of explanation. You can't come in here, bleed all over my floor and expect me to shrug and wave as you walk out the door."

"Maira cleaned all the blood off the floor."

"Kade!"

"Shh." He put a hand over her mouth, his other grasping her shoulder. "I don't want your family in here asking questions too."

Amber twisted out of his grip. "Then tell me what's going on."

"I'm sorry. I can't." He turned to go again.

Amber took a deep breath, ready to scream. She barely managed a second worth of sound before his hand was over her mouth. He'd moved in a blur of speed to stop her. This time she could only glare at him.

"Would you rather I tied and gagged you so we can leave without you calling anyone?"

Amber could barely shake her head.

"If I take my hand away, will you scream?"

She shook her head again. As soon as he removed his hand she demanded, "Why can't you tell me what's going on? You were the one who landed on my balcony, walked in and demanded I lock the doors behind you. I deserve to know."

"I'll think about it."

Amber searched his face carefully. She couldn't tell what he thought or if he told the truth. "Are you saying that so you can get out of here without me screaming the place down? Or are you actually considering answering me?"

Kade grinned. "No. It depends on other things." He started to move away again.

"What other things?" Amber followed him to the French doors that were open again. She noticed his friends stood on the balcony.

"Don't you have to shower and see your mother?"

Amber shrugged. "She'll come and hassle me again if I take too long."

"That's what I'm afraid of," Kade muttered. He reached out and grabbed hold of the curtain that hung at the French doors. With a quick movement, he spun it around her.

Amber struggled to free herself. The moment she escaped, she stepped out onto the balcony and glanced around, looking for the three of them. She peered over the rails, her gaze scanning the ground. Having nowhere else to look, she studied the sky. In the distance she saw three large… Amber's mind struggled with the word bird. But what else could she call a creature that flew through the air, propelled forward with large wings? She laughed nervously. Prehistoric bird? Dragon? Mutated bird of prey? She had no idea.

Closing the French doors, she made sure she locked

them. It was the first time since she'd been here. Her room was on the second storey of the house. She'd thought she was safe. It wasn't like it was a major city or anything. A shudder went through her as she recalled the past six nights she'd slept with the doors unlocked. She drew the curtains together and turned away from the doors. It took her several minutes before she could make herself walk to the bathroom.

After a quick shower, Amber stepped out of her room and walked towards the other end of the corridor. She passed two closed doors that were next to each other and opposite the stairs. From habit, she tried each doorknob as she passed. They were still locked. The only comment about them she could get from her grandmother was that if she hadn't been so nosey she wouldn't have known they were locked. Her mother's room was the last one. She knocked on the door. When there was no answer, she knocked again.

"Mum?" Amber opened the door a fraction when there was still no reply. Her mother lay on her side, one hand under her cheek, still dressed and on top of the quilt. She was fast asleep. Amber carefully closed the door, relieved she didn't have to endure the discussion. It was probably yet another one about her attitude. She was sick of those conversations. Who wouldn't have an attitude when they'd been ripped from the life they loved with absolutely no say in the matter.

Returning to her room, Amber locked her bedroom door then flicked the light switch off so only the bedside lamp lit the room. Pulling back the sheets on the queen-sized bed in the middle of the room, she flopped onto it, rolling onto her back. Her gaze was drawn to the curtains that covered the French doors and she sat up in annoyance. There was no way she'd be able to sleep. She had too many unanswered questions.

Her gaze travelled around the room. Clothes spilled from a built-in wardrobe that wasn't quite shut, a suitcase open on the floor beside it only half unpacked. Her schoolbag sat by the door, books in a precarious tower near it and a hairbrush, clips, scarves and hair ties overwhelmed a duchess. In the middle was a crystal tray on a frilly piece of embroidery with two crystal containers. A laptop sat closed on a desk in the corner. Amber's gaze came to a stop on her laptop. She frowned and glanced at her door. Her mother was asleep and her grandmother never came upstairs since her bedroom was downstairs.

Within seconds, Amber was in front of her laptop and signing into her messenger to check who was online. She frowned when she saw both Crystal and Josh go offline. Her brother and Angela, another school friend, were still online. She ignored the rest of the people listed as online, since she only knew them through games. Maybe her brother would know the secret her mother was keeping from her.

Amber says: Miss me yet?

Jay says: Who's this?

Amber says: Ha, ha, very funny.

Jay says: :)

Amber says: What's mum meant to tell me?

Jay says: How would I know?

Amber says: Her and the witch were yelling and I heard the witch say something about her not having told me something.

Jay says: Could be anything.

Amber says: Took you ages to reply to that. You sure you don't know something?

Jay says: You sure you don't?

Amber says: What's that supposed to mean?

Jay says: How long you planning on staying with Grandma?

Amber says: As short a time as possible.

Jay says: Really?

Amber says: What gives?

Jay says: g2g.

Amber says: Jay!!!!

Jay says: Pay more attention. And I didn't say anything.

Amber says: You haven't said anything. Stupid cryptic comments.

Jay says: Can't spell this one out for you. Gotta figure it out for yourself.

Amber says: Fine! Have you seen Crys and Josh about? Never seem to be able to get hold of them lately.

Jay says: Both of them???

Amber says: Didn't I just say that?

Jay says: Hmmm.

Amber says: Spit it out.

Jay says: They avoiding you? You're normally chatting away to them every night.

Amber says: Why would they be avoiding me? Not like I wanted to move here.

Jay says: Are you sure we're related?

Amber says: Some days I really hope not!

Jay says: g2g.

Amber says: You trying to avoid me?

Jay says: No. Bed calling. Some of us actually try and pay attention in class and not use it as sleeping time.

Amber says: K. Later.

Jay says: Night.

Chapter Three

Amber exited the window and checked to see if Angela was still online. Relieved to see she was, she clicked on her name. Maybe she could give her some answers. No one else seemed to be interested in telling her anything.

Amber says: Where is everyone lately?

Snowflake… or just a flake says: I'm right here :)

Amber says: Hi everyone! How about Crys and Josh? They never seem to be about.

Snowflake… or just a flake says: Guess they're busy.

Amber says: But you see them at school, right?

Snowflake… or just a flake says: Of course.

Amber says: They said anything? I've sent them all types of messages and heard nothing back.

Snowflake… or just a flake says: They haven't talked to you at all?

Amber says: No.

Snowflake… or just a flake says: Guess they must be busy.

Amber says: Come on Inge. Spill!

Snowflake… or just a flake says: I've got nothing to spill.

Amber says: Inge!!

Snowflake… or just a flake says: They said they'd talk to you. You have any voice messages on your phone? Texts?

Amber says: Nothing. It's like they've dropped off the face of the Earth.

Amber says: Disappeared.

Amber says: Were abducted by aliens.

Amber says: Kidnapped by Bigfoot.

Snowflake… or just a flake says: I get the drift. No need for more scenarios.

Amber says: And I was just getting warmed up!

Snowflake… or just a flake says: g2g.

Amber says: NO!

Snowflake… or just a flake says: My mum just told me lights out.

Amber says: Talk to me. I need to know what's going on.

Snowflake... or just a flake says: Have you rung them?

Amber says: Yes. And sent a million texts. Come on! You know what's happening. I'll keep ringing you all night if you don't tell me. You won't get any sleep.

Snowflake... or just a flake says: We were at a party Friday night.

Amber says: The day I left! You didn't pine for me for long.

Snowflake... or just a flake says: You want to hear this or not?

Amber says: Yes.

Snowflake... or just a flake says: They'd had a couple of drinks. I didn't think it was many, but maybe they'd had more than I thought. Next thing I look over and they're kissing like lovers separated for a decade.

Snowflake... or just a flake says: You still there?

Snowflake... or just a flake says: Hello?

Amber says: Are you sure?

Snowflake... or just a flake says: Of course I am.

Amber says: Absolutely?

Snowflake... or just a flake says: I told them they should tell you before you found out some other way. I can't believe they thought you wouldn't suspect something when they don't talk to you for a week. Well, as good as a week.

Snowflake… or just a flake says: Still there?

Amber says: Yeah.

Snowflake… or just a flake says: I didn't want to be the one to tell you.

Amber says: I know.

Snowflake… or just a flake says: I'm sorry.

Snowflake… or just a flake says: You've gone quiet again. Can I go now? Before Mum grounds me.

Amber says: Thanks Inge. Sorry to hassle you about it.

Snowflake… or just a flake says: No problem. Sorry they didn't tell you and you had to hear it from me.

Amber says: Night.

Snowflake… or just a flake says: Night.

Amber stared at the screen. She wanted to write a message begging them to tell her it was all lies. But they hadn't spoken to her in six days. Unheard of. Completely and utterly unheard of. Crystal would only avoid her because of something major. Josh she wasn't so sure about. He'd only been her boyfriend for two months.

She sent a message to Josh first. He was good

looking, could kiss better than anyone else she'd ever kissed and outgoing. But he was only a boyfriend, their history short. The message only needed to be equally as short. She typed 'We're over.' and sent it. She frowned as she thought about what to write to Crystal. After many tries, she finally had a message she could send.

Amber says: We became best friends on the first day of grade one and no matter what happened we were always there for each other. I thought we were closer than sisters. I was obviously wrong. I hope he's worth it because I don't know that I'll ever be able to forgive you. Not that you stole him. That I probably could have forgiven. But that you hid from me and avoided me. All you needed to do was say two words and I probably would have forgiven you. Now, 'I'm sorry' is far too late in coming.

Amber closed her laptop down. She slowly rose and walked over to the bed to sit on the edge of it. She felt numb. No. Made of lead. Could lead bleed? It felt like someone had shredded her chest, from the inside. Like the same creature that had attacked Kade had ripped her apart. Her wounds would not be so easily sewn back together.

She lay down and turned the light out, staring unseeing at the ceiling. "I want to go home," she whispered into the dark. Just like every other time she'd spoken it since coming here, no one listened to her.

* * *

The wind whistled past as Amber worked her wings harder. The scent on the breeze drew her on. Excitement rushed through her veins as quickly as the wind cut past her. Her eyes narrowed as she spotted the deer grazing peacefully in the moonlight. Claws outstretched, she swooped down. At the last second, the deer tried to bound away. But she'd left it too long. A sharp shake as she flew higher killed the doe instantly. The doe hung limp and heavy. Still warm.

The smell of blood swirled around her as claws pierced the hide. Her mouth watered. She looked around for somewhere safe to eat. A place where she wouldn't be disturbed. Then she had company. They swooped in on either side of her. A glance showed they were friends. To the right was a black scaled dragon with silver wing veins and green eyes shot through with silver. On her left flew a slightly larger dragon, dark velvet brown, deep blue wing veins and slightly darker blue eyes.

"You going to share?" The dragon on the right didn't talk with her mouth, but used her mind. And she had Maira's voice.

* * *

Amber sat up with a jolt. Adrenaline rushed through her body. She could still smell the blood, feel the wind and the weight of the carcass. She flexed her fingers, surprised to find they weren't claws. Checking the time on her alarm clock, she saw it wasn't quite four in the morning. Dropping back onto her pillow, she groaned. She should be asleep, not thinking about tearing a deer carcass apart and feeding on it. She shuddered. It wasn't like she was a vegetarian. She loved a thick rump fried in the pan, or any cut of meat for that matter. As long as it was cooked. Completely cooked. Not even slightly pink. The thought of eating raw meat, including hide and bones, made her feel a little ill. And yet she also had a slight craving for it. Leftover from the dream. At least she hoped it was leftover from the dream.

No wonder she hated change. You alter one thing

and it screwed everything up. This was all her grandmother's fault, breaking her arm so her mother dragged her away from home. Her friends were hours away, the bed she now slept in was nowhere near as comfortable as her own and she'd started having nightmares. She guessed her grandmother didn't only give little kids nightmares.

"Go to sleep, you idiot," Amber muttered. The words didn't help. Sleep took ages to return.

* * *

Amber hurried along the school corridor, turned a corner and stopped abruptly. She saw Kade, back to her, facing Flinn, someone she'd been told to avoid. Flinn had short brown hair, blue eyes and was reasonably good looking. Nothing to make you stare or look at twice, or so you'd think. But something about him made you give him as much space as possible. Amber didn't know if it was the way he held himself, the look in his eyes or the tone of his voice when he spoke. It didn't matter. Instinct kicked in and she froze, unwilling to take another step. She could see the door of her classroom several metres past them, but class could wait.

Flinn put his hands against Kade's shoulders and pushed at him. Kade didn't budge. Instead, his hands came up and he pushed against Flinn. Brann appeared at their side, coming from the classroom Amber needed to enter. There was more whispered conversation, but it was no less furious for all its quietness. They separated, angry glances at Brann. Then Flinn looked up and saw Amber standing, watching them.

"What are you looking at?" Flinn started to stride towards her.

Kade grabbed Flinn by the arm and spun him back to face him. Amber took the opportunity to hurry towards the classroom, keeping close to the wall furthest from Flinn. She couldn't hear what Kade said, but she noticed Flinn shook his arm off before he spat out his own comment. He turned to glare at Amber before he strode away.

Amber stopped, her gaze on Kade, ignoring Brann who wandered back into class. Her gaze darted to Kade's shoulder, hidden by his shirt, before meeting his gaze again. "How are you?"

Kade continued to stare at her a moment longer. "It'd be better if you stayed away from us." He turned and entered the classroom.

Anger rushed through her. It wasn't like she'd

asked him to sit by her side for the rest of the day. It had been a simple question. She crossed the last few steps to the classroom and stopped in the doorway when she saw the only seat left was next to Kade. He glared at her. She couldn't resist a slight smile as she slowly walked towards the seat and made a production of sitting and getting comfortable. Kade's lips thinned with each deliberate glance his way. She didn't even bother trying to stop her smile from widening. It served him right. It wouldn't have hurt him to be civil.

"Books out." Mrs Thornley, the English teacher, stepped into the room. "Who can recap what we discussed last class?" Her gaze scanned the room and she pointed to one of the eager students with their hands in the air.

Amber ignored the droning voice as she glanced at Kade who caught her look and glared at her. She barely managed to stifle a giggle, but preventing another smile from forming was too much effort. Tearing a piece of paper from her notebook, she was about to write a note to him when the atmosphere started to change.

There was a hum in the air like something was about to happen. Amber frowned and noticed most of the class seemed oblivious. Except Kade and Brann.

The hum intensified until it was nearly a crackle and she rubbed her arms, trying to rid herself of the uncomfortable sensation filling them. Kade glanced at the clock on the wall before he stared out the window.

"Flinn went after the Pliethin. I saw him from my classroom window," Maira said.

Amber looked around. It had been like Maira had stood beside her. Yet she wasn't even in this class. She frowned. *"What's a plea-thin?"*

"Block!" Kade yelled.

She reached up to grab her head, which seemed like it might explode from his shout, as the world seemed to collapse in on her.

Chapter Four

Amber struggled to sit up. She brushed aside Kade's hand as he tried to help. Mrs Thornley peered anxiously at her while she kept shooing students back to their seats. Amber looked around at the curious faces as she got up off the floor, dusting off her clothes with her hands. She swayed unsteadily.

"Do you need to go to the sick room?" Mrs Thornley asked.

Amber shrugged. "I don't know. I think I just need some fresh air." What she really needed was to ask Kade what was going on.

"I'll go with her. In case she faints again." Kade put an arm around her waist.

When Amber tried to elbow him away, he tightened his grip. If it wasn't for the fact she wanted answers, she would have protested his suggestion.

"Well…"

"I'll take her to the sick room if she isn't feeling any better after a few minutes." Kade started to usher Amber towards the door before Mrs Thornley could say anything. Eventually she nodded and the two of them stepped into the hall.

"What's going on?" Amber demanded as soon as they were alone.

"No need to thank me for catching you before you hit the floor," Kade said.

"Thank you! Why should I when you had something to do with it?"

Kade hurried her towards the doors leading outside, where he tried to deposit her on a bench under a shady tree. "I'll come back shortly and check on you."

"No you won't. You'll tell me what's going on, now." Amber ignored the bench she wanted to collapse onto. Her legs felt unsteady but she refused to let them give out. There were so many questions she wanted answered, including ones she had from last night.

"I don't have time. There's something I need to deal with."

She was tempted to argue, but doubted she'd be able to change his mind. "Promise me you'll come back and answer my questions. Swear it."

"Amber-"

"No!"

"How about you get one question that I have to answer truthfully?"

"Five."

"Two and that's it. Any longer and I won't need to take off."

"Fine. Two. And you try and get out of answering them I'll tell everyone about you landing on my roof." Amber held out her hand. Kade hurriedly shook it and took off at a run. The crackle was still in the air and Amber dropped onto the bench. Now she had to figure out which questions would give her the most answers.

She hadn't worked out what she should ask by the time the bell rang for class. Kade also hadn't returned. Amber reluctantly wandered to her next class, her mind far from the classroom and what the teacher said. She was glad when the bell rang for lunch.

Amber wandered around the school, looking for Kade. She only found Maira who sat with two other girls from their art class. She couldn't recall their names.

She waited impatiently for Maira to finish speaking to her companions. "I'm looking for Kade."

"I don't know where he is."

"Then you can give him a message from me. Tell him I want his answers by midnight or they don't count." She was sick of secrets. If only she could figure out a way to learn the one her mother was keeping without letting her know she'd overheard her.

Maira rose to her feet. Her chair scraped loudly across the floor. "Look-"

"Don't start with me." Amber pointed a finger at Maira. "Midnight." She spun away, headed for her locker. If she'd been at her old school, there would've been a number of people she could have sat with. Here she had no one willing to spend time with her. She ignored the smile sent her way from one of the guys from her maths class. Okay, maybe she should rephrase that to include no one she wanted to spend time with either. She glared at him and he turned away.

Not knowing what else to do after she'd eaten, Amber decided to go to the library and see if there was a computer free so she could check her emails and messages. She would have used her phone, but she'd nearly used up all her data allowance for the month. By the time it was her turn the bell rang. Ignoring it, she quickly signed in. There were no messages and she felt like the day had been one disaster after another. Once she'd signed out, she rose, glaring at the computer screen for a moment before she strode to her next class.

Amber wished she could go home, her real home, not her grandmother's home. She wanted to confront Crystal. The rest of her classes were spent planning various ways to accomplish that. She wished she was seventeen already and had her license, but that was still two months away. And a bus would take too long. It had to be a trip she could make in the space of a day. There was no way her mother was going to let her go home, even to talk to Crystal. She drew in the margin of her book. First a sports car, a figure vaguely looking like her at the wheel. Then herself in a hang glider. She frowned as she noticed the wings were almost draconic.

Kade still hadn't appeared by the time she returned home. The rest of the day dragged. There were no messages, emails, or phone calls. There was nothing for her to do other than homework. She reluctantly sat at her desk and started it, almost relieved when her mother interrupted.

"I thought you were going to come and see me last night once you were finished in the bathroom." Donna hovered in the doorway.

Amber leaned back in her chair. Her relief had

lasted for all of two seconds. "You were asleep. Practically snoring."

Donna stared at the floor. "It's not so bad here, is it?"

"I hate it."

"I thought we could stay here so you could see the school year out. You're right, it probably isn't fair to shift you again."

Amber leapt to her feet. "No!" She wished now she'd thought to lock her bedroom door and not answer her mother's knock.

"Now Amber-"

"No." Amber's jaw dropped as the situation suddenly became clear, Jay's cryptic comments making sense. "You never had any intention of going home again. It was all a trick. You've left Dad!"

"I wouldn't exactly say that."

"Then what would you say? Are you going back to him?"

"I don't know." Donna paused. "It's complicated. When you're an adult-"

"Don't pull the 'you wouldn't understand' comment on me. You won't let me use it."

"That's different. I was a teenager. I can understand what you're going through. You've never been an adult."

Amber turned away and dropped back into her chair. "I've got homework to do." She stared determinedly at the screen of her laptop. If she had to hear one more piece of bad news, she might start screaming. Very loudly and for a very long time. Like a siren.

"Amber…"

Amber refused to acknowledge her mother. She listened as Donna sighed heavily, closed the door and walked away. As soon as she heard the door shut, she hurried over and locked it.

She took one step towards her laptop then changed her mind. Walking to her bed she dropped down to lay on her back, arms spread as she stared sightlessly at the ceiling. Her mind was blank. Deliberately so. She didn't want to think. Not yet. Too much had happened at once. And none of it good. Life wasn't normally like that. She knew she often coasted through life, skimming the surface. But that was her choice. She didn't want life to be too deep. That usually meant pain. She'd seen what emotional pain did to people. She wasn't an idiot. There was no need to experience something to learn about it. You only had to watch what happened to those around you. Her grandmother was a perfect example of what happened when you lost someone you loved. No way was she going to turn out like her. As friendly as a red-bellied black snake and probably as poisonous.

Time ticked away without her. She ignored the knock on her door. Her mother tried to insist it was time for dinner, but Amber acted deaf. Even the knock much later, and her mother insisting it was time for bed, was ignored. She continued to stare at the ceiling, only the bedside lamp and laptop screen lighting the room. Pushing thoughts away about her present, she focused on the past. Parties. Sleepovers with Crystal. Whispering and laughing in the dark with Crystal. Always Crystal. She couldn't picture a single moment of her life that hadn't involved Crystal since the first day of school. They'd been closer than Siamese twins. That was why she couldn't understand. How could Crystal have done that to her when they'd been so close?

A knock at the French doors caught her attention. Amber forced herself to her feet. Checking her alarm clock showed her it was after eleven. The moment the door was opened, Kade stepped into the room. He wore leather pants, boots of a similar material and his chest was bare.

After a lingering look at his chest, Amber's gaze went to his shoulder. Reaching out, her fingers lightly traced the faint scars left on his skin. She tried to comprehend the impossible. Even the stitches were gone. She met Kade's gaze when his hand captured hers, holding it centimetres from the warmth of his skin.

"Kade-"

"You said you wanted answers before midnight. Better ask your questions then."

She hesitated. She had so many more questions to ask than the two she was allowed. One sprang to mind she hadn't even considered earlier. "What did you do last night after you left me?"

"I went hunting." He released her hand.

"That's not a proper answer. You need to at least add who with and what you were hunting."

"I was with Maira and Brann and I hunted deer."

Goosebumps rose on Amber's arms as she stared at Kade. She closed her eyes as her dream rushed in on her. Sight, sound, smell, taste. Opening her eyes, she met Kade's gaze, holding it a moment before she spoke. "Are you a dragon?"

Kade swore, turning away from her. "Ask a different one. That isn't a proper question."

"That's the one I want answered. You said you'd answer two questions. That's my second one."

"What made you ask that?"

"A dream and your first answer."

Kade looked shocked. "You were with me last night? I didn't feel you."

"Only in my dreams. Okay. I'll ask a different question since you've pretty much answered that one with all your drama."

"Amber, you can't even think that."

"What? That you're a dragon?"

"Forget everything you've seen, heard or think you know. It'd be safer for you."

"I want to know everything that's going on."

"That isn't a question. Hurry up and ask your second question. I have to go."

"What's a Pliethin?"

Kade closed his eyes momentarily. When he opened them, his eyes were almost gold. "Energy. A creature of energy."

"Did you get it? Or did Flinn?"

"You're out of questions." Kade turned back to the French doors and started to step through them.

Amber recalled the way it had felt to have someone speak in her mind and how she'd thought when she'd spoken in their mind. She gathered her energy. *"Kade! Don't-"*

Kade was a blur of motion, not halting until he had both hands around her upper arms. "Stop."

"Or what? You'll cause me to pass out again?"

"That was an accident. We've never blocked a human mind before. We used too much force. I'm sorry. Just please don't broadcast to every dragon in the area that you can hear them."

"Why?"

"Because you're not meant to know we exist."

"It was the blood, wasn't it?"

Kade stared at her for a moment before he nodded. "It'll wear off. Two to four weeks and everything will be back to normal."

"No it won't, because I'll know you're real."

"Forget about us."

"Us?" She thought about her dream. "Are Maira and Brann dragons too?"

"Amber!"

Amber's mouth rounded as another possibility occurred to her. "Is Flinn a dragon?"

"You're out of questions, remember?"

Amber's eyes narrowed. "Show me what you look like as a dragon and I'll stop asking questions tonight."

"No. And no more broadcasting either."

"Broadcasting?"

"Speaking with your mind so everyone in the area can hear you."

"Show me what you look like as a dragon and I won't broadcast tonight either."

"Don't be stupid. There are worse creatures than dragons to notice you exist."

"Like what?"

Kade shook his head. "Enough questions."

"Then show me what you look like as a dragon."

Amber barely had time to finish her sentence when the air around Kade shimmered and his body seemed to flow into that of a dragon, giving him the bulk of an elephant, but only the height of a large horse. He was a golden brown dragon with gold wing veins and tawny eyes shot through with gold. She stared at him, her mouth ajar.

She managed to close her mouth and take a step forward. Reaching out, she tentatively placed her hand against the warm scales on his chest. She was fascinated. It was like one of the fairytales, her father had read to her as a child, suddenly come to life. Her fingers trailed across his chest. He lowered his head so his gaze could meet hers. She reached up to touch his face, the warm scales smooth under her hand, except where they overlapped the next. Kade moved forward, flowing back into a human as he did. Amber's hand rested against his jaw and his arms went around her.

"As a dragon I can still feel when you touch me."

Amber ran her hand down his neck, continuing downwards until she stopped at his chest, palm pressed against his heartbeat. "Can you feel it as strongly when you have scales?"

"No." His voice was barely a whisper.

"What does-"

"I have to go." When Amber opened her mouth to speak again, Kade shook his head. "You promised." He stepped back, his arms dropping to his sides. "No broadcasting."

Before Amber could say anything, he walked out the door. She hurried after him, stepping onto the balcony. He was gone. Looking upwards, she found him. Wings beating strongly, rapidly taking him into the distance until she could no longer see him. And still she stood there, staring up.

He'd said there were worse creatures than dragons. Did they have wings too? Sighing, she headed back inside, turned off her laptop and flopped onto her bed. Her hand closed and she recalled the feel of his scales. A moment of doubt surfaced. Did mental illness run in her family? No. He'd felt too real. Warm and real. She wasn't crazy.

Chapter Five

Amber tore herself from the nightmare, struggling to sit up. Her breath came in gasps as she reached for the bedside lamp to dispel the dark. The eyes were not so easy to get rid of. Blood red eyes had stared at her like she was the next feast. She tried to make herself believe it was a dream, even going so far as to say the words out loud. It didn't help. She threw back the bed sheets and rose to pace the floor. She knew she wouldn't be able to sleep again. Nightmares didn't normally bother her, but this one had seemed so real. Like she'd open her eyes and some creature would be lurking in the corner of her room watching her, waiting for her to move before he pounced and tore her apart.

Pulling on jeans, a shirt and a jacket, she grabbed socks, her boots and her backpack style handbag before heading downstairs to the front door. Quietly letting herself out, she pulled on her socks and boots and then glanced around before heading down the streetlight lit bitumen. She slipped her arms through the straps of her handbag, barely giving her grandmother's two-storey brick house a glance. It was the ugliest house on the block and the two balconies looked like they'd been an afterthought. One was at the side of the house at her room, the other at the front of the house.

The sound of her boots against the street echoed in the quiet morning. It made her look over her shoulder nervously. She took her mobile phone from her handbag and checked the time. Daylight was about an hour and a half away. No wonder she felt unnerved. Back home there'd be cars speeding down the streets, groups of people about and a steady stream of noise. Here it was far too still and unnaturally quiet. A nice friendly, quiet country town. Just what she didn't need. Give her a noisy city any time.

She turned the corner. A streetlight ahead of her flickered off and on. Starting to feel uncomfortable, her gaze searched the area again. She was still alone. Her footsteps hit the bitumen faster as her gaze continued to dart everywhere. She didn't feel alone. She felt like something watched her. Turning to go back to her grandmother's home, the sound of air whooshing above her made her look up. A dark shadow came at her and she saw the glint of two outstretched claws and red eyes.

Amber screamed. She spun and ran. Home wasn't an option. A street over she heard a dog bark. Running to the footpath, she hoped the trees would slow the creature down. Her breath came in sharp gasps and her hand pressed against her side where a stitch had developed.

A harsh cry above and behind her caused her to stumble. Glancing back, she dodged behind the trunk of a large tree. She didn't know what type of tree, she was only relieved it hadn't lost its leaves like some of the other trees had when the weather had started to grow cooler.

"Kade!" She desperately tried to call out to him, mind to mind. Was this the other creature he'd talked about?

"What do you think-"

She clearly pictured what she ran from, weaving amongst the trees on the footpath. She hoped he could see the picture she sent.

"A wyvern! Where are you?"

Relief rushed over her, but she didn't slow. She pictured where she was, her gaze darting around as she concentrated on running, ignoring the pain that made her want to double over. Her hand pressed harder into her side.

"Don't stop running. We're coming."

She didn't know how much longer she could keep moving. *"Hurry."*

Time seemed to drag out, but only minutes passed before three shadowy dragons swooped out of the sky and attacked the wyvern. Amber collapsed onto the grass and her breath came in harsh gasps. Brushing tears from her eyes, she tried to see what was happening in the skies above her. Her hand pressed against the side she lay on, unable to move.

With a last screech, the wyvern fled. The three dragons gave pursuit. When Amber thought they might leave her alone, one turned and flew back to her. He landed on the ground and knelt beside her in human form.

Kade reached out to her, a hand on her shoulder, pulling her into a sitting position. "It didn't get you?"

Amber could only shake her head.

"You're sure?" He ran his hands over her arms, then her back.

She threw her arms around him and he folded his around her. "What was it?" Her breathing started to return to normal. Her heart continued to race and the stitch was there, painful when she moved, but it had started to ease.

"Wyvern."

"Why'd it attack me?"

"It's the natural enemy of dragons."

"I'm not a dragon."

"No. But it would have smelt the dragon blood in you. As little as it is, the wyvern would have thought you were a young dragon. An unprotected, young dragon. Easy game." Kade tensed and started to pull away from her.

Amber clung to him. "Don't-" Her eyes widened as she saw another dragon swoop in to land beside them. She let Kade stand, as the dark blue dragon with gold wing veins became Flinn.

"I heard her broadcast. What do you think you're doing?" Flinn stalked towards Kade to stand toe to toe.

"None of your business."

"It's my business if she tries to expose us. What the hell were you thinking?"

Amber struggled to her feet. She'd fight her own battles and defend herself. Even against a dragon. "Why would I tell anyone? They'd medicate me and I'd be stuck seeing a shrink for years."

Flinn ignored her. "What happens if she's killed by

a wyvern? You can't be seen with her. I'll get rid of her myself if you're going to be that stupid."

"Back off, Flinn."

Flinn grinned maliciously. "The Elders would be interested in this development."

Kade grabbed Flinn by the throat and his voice dropped menacingly. "You speak of this and you'll regret every syllable."

"Kade!" Amber grabbed his arm. She might as well have tried to move a boulder.

"You always fought for the wrong things, brother."

Kade released him instantly. "You only call on the bond when it's convenient." He took a step back. "And you fight far too many battles, Flinn. Brotherhood won't help you if you fight the wrong one."

"Get rid of her before she causes more problems." Flinn turned, leapt into the air, changing into a dragon in mid leap. His wings beat hard and he shot into the sky.

Amber stared after Flinn, momentarily speechless. "He's your brother?"

"Not in the human sense."

"Then what sense?"

"We trained together. It's a lineage thing."

"I don't know anything about your... ah... people?"

Kade smiled fleetingly. "Gold Warriors. We're descended from our first king. Only we can capture the Pliethin or hold positions of power."

"Gold? As in the colour on your wings?"

Kade nodded. He glanced around. "Let's get you home before daylight. It's not too far off."

"That's right, you can't be seen with me in case I come to a messy end. We don't want a finger pointed at you now, do we?" Amber glared at him.

"Amber." He sighed heavily. "Don't be difficult about this."

"What attacked you the night you landed on my balcony?"

Kade hesitated. "A wyvern."

"So even you can't beat one on your own."

"I was distracted or it wouldn't have got me." He started to walk towards her home.

Amber hurried along at his side. She forced her aching legs to move. "What distracted you?"

"Why aren't you scared and screaming?"

"Because I'm trying to take my mind off it by grilling you." She waited for Kade to answer. Her thoughts were distracted by the leather pants and boots he wore.

"I'll answer some of your questions if you promise not to approach me at school."

"Why leather?"

"Huh?"

Amber's fingers brushed lightly against the waist of his pants. "Leather. I noticed even Flinn wears them."

"You didn't answer me."

"About?"

Kade sighed. "Stay away from me at school and I'll answer some of your questions."

Amber froze and Kade stopped to turn and look at her. "You think it's going to get me, don't you?"

"I don't know. But I can't take chances with the lives of my people."

"Your people?"

"Brann and Maira."

"You… you own them?" Amber frowned.

Kade shook his head. "No. I'm responsible for them."

"Why?"

"If you want me to walk you home you have to get there before daybreak."

Amber's gaze was drawn to the sky. Already it was lightening. The thought of walking home alone made her shudder. The thought of walking the rest of the way home made her aching limbs feel weak.

The slight tremble that had been in them ever since her race from the wyvern increased and it took all her willpower not to let her knees buckle.

Kade swore. "Why didn't you tell me?" He shimmered and transformed into a dragon. *"Get on."*

"What?"

Kade nudged her towards his back with his head. He held his foreleg close to his body and she used it like a step so she could swing her leg over his broad back. There was nowhere to hold on.

"I'll fall off."

"Hold on with your legs."

The trembling in her legs increased as she tightened them. She couldn't help the soft shriek that escaped as Kade took to the sky. What had taken her ages to cross, took Kade less than a minute. He partially perched on the rail of the balcony, his wings still in motion, and Amber slid off him. Her legs gave way and she expected to hit the floor. At the last second, Kade became human and his arms wrapped around her, dragging her upright.

She let herself lean against him for a moment. For a few seconds she considered taking up a sport so she'd be in better condition. She mentally laughed at herself. She knew she'd be looking for excuses to get out of attending from the first day. Reluctantly she pulled away from Kade, opening the French doors. She didn't know if she should be relieved she'd forgotten to lock them or annoyed any creature could have entered her room while she slept.

When Kade followed her into the bedroom, Amber turned to face him. "You can go. I don't need a babysitter."

"I'll be back at dark. Leave your doors unlocked for me." He gestured towards the French doors.

"Why?"

"Because wyverns won't show their face in daylight where people live. They've come in contact with your weapons. After dark… then you'll need protection."

"Can't you get it out of me?"

"What?"

"The blood."

Kade shook his head. "No. But I won't leave you alone. I won't let my mistake cost you your life. From dusk to dawn there'll be someone with you. And any time you want to go somewhere sparsely populated."

"How am I going to explain that? I barely know anyone here and the next second I have you shadowing me. That'll go down real well with my mum."

"We'll take turns."

"I don't know."

"Here or at our place."

"Is there a responsible adult there?" Amber laughed sharply when Kade shook his head. "Then I've probably got no chance of staying."

Kade reached out and took her hand. "I'm sorry I brought this to you."

Amber pulled away from him. "You know where the door is." She walked into her bathroom and closed the door, fighting the urge to cry. Her body ached, her nightmare was real and she wanted to go home. Her home. She thought of her father and Crystal. But even that was changing. Just like everything else.

Quickly stripping off her clothes, she stood under the shower, leaning against the wall. She desperately tried to stay on her feet as the water streamed over her. It didn't help one bit. Her body still ached and she missed home more than ever. Turning off the taps, she stepped out of the shower, dried herself and grabbed the short, black robe that hung on the back of the door. Tying the sash, she stepped into her room, freezing. Kade sat at her desk, having turned the chair to face the room.

"Why are you still here?"

"You looked ready to collapse."

"When you leave, I will."

"I wanted to make sure you managed to get to your bed okay."

"Why? Are you planning on tucking me in?" There was a sharp edge to her voice.

Kade rose to his feet with a chuckle. "Only if you need me to."

Amber glanced between him and her bed. She crossed her arms. "I'm tired, exhausted and cranky." Not to mention homesick. "Go home and leave me alone."

"When you're safe in bed."

"Fine!" Amber strode to her bed, dropped on it and pulled the linen over her. She'd planned to dress in her sleep shirt first, but she changed her mind since Kade was in the room. "Now out."

Kade walked towards the bed. "Didn't you mention something about tucking you in?"

Amber sat up. "Don't you dare."

Kade smiled slightly. "Sweet dreams." He bent forward and brushed his lips against hers. "Call me at the slightest danger." He handed her a piece of paper with a phone number on it. "No matter the hour."

Before Amber could reply, he was gone, the French doors closing softly behind him. She looked down at the number clutched in her hand and wondered why she couldn't call to him with her mind. Flinn and the wyvern knew she existed, so what did it matter?

Chapter Six

A knock on the bedroom door startled Amber to wakefulness. She sat up, surprised she'd been able to fall asleep again. The knock became more impatient.

"What?"

"It's nearly ten. Are you planning to sleep all of Saturday?" Donna spoke through the door.

"Yeah. So quit trying to wake me. The less time I have to be awake in Hicksville, the better." It was probably her safest option. At least until the dragon blood wore off.

"Amber-"

"Goodnight." Amber lay back down and listened carefully. Eventually she heard her mother's footsteps recede. She tried to close her eyes and go back to sleep. It was impossible.

Flinging the bed sheets aside, she quickly dressed in jeans and a shirt, pulled on her boots and, once she'd entered Kade's number in the contact list, pushed her phone into her pocket. She considered heading down for breakfast, but didn't want to face her mother or grandmother yet. Instead, she turned on her laptop and checked for messages. There were several, but none from Crystal. She didn't know whether to be annoyed or relieved. She opted for annoyed.

Once she'd replied to her messages, she had no choice other than to go downstairs for something to eat. Her stomach felt like it pressed against her spine and she felt a little light headed. She didn't know if that was from hunger or her early morning run. And to think people actually enjoyed running. Amber slowly shook her head as she wandered downstairs and into the kitchen.

A glance around showed her she was alone. It took only minutes to throw together a sandwich, scribble a note and put it under a fridge magnet. She considered grabbing her handbag from her bedroom, but when a check of the lounge room showed it was empty, she slipped out the front door instead, hurrying down the street.

She'd nearly finished her sandwich when she stopped suddenly and spun to look behind her. A hand went to her hip as she glared at Maira who was a couple of houses back. She finished off her sandwich as she stood and watched Maira.

After standing there, staring at her for a minute, Maira seemed to come to a decision. She strode towards Amber. As Maira reached her side, Amber noticed she wore the same chunky silver and black bracelets she'd worn when she came to help Kade. They were tight on her skin, almost like they were a part of it. Amber squashed the urge to reach out and touch them. She also forced her mind away from the jewellery and back to her initial annoyance.

"Why are you following me?"

Maira shrugged. "Got me beat."

"Then go home."

Maira shook her head and silver earrings bounced at her ears. "Can't."

"Why not?"

"Because a good soldier always follows orders."

"Soldier… Kade…" Amber frowned. "He's older than you?"

Maira laughed. "Barely. By a month. But that's not how it works. It's the bloodline. Anyway, that's unimportant. My orders are to shadow you, his words, and protect you. He said there was a good chance you'd wander off into unpopulated areas without telling him."

Amber turned back in the direction she'd been headed before the uncomfortable sensation of being watched had made her turn around. She'd thought it might be a wyvern, even though Kade had said they didn't hunt during daylight. Striding silently along the footpath, she tried to ignore Maira who continued to walk beside her. Who did Kade think he was? She didn't need a babysitter. It was daylight.

"So what are we going to do?" Silence greeted Maira's words. "I guess it doesn't matter, I'll find out soon enough. Not that there's much in this direction. You don't strike me as the type to be headed to the park. Not to play on the swings anyway."

Amber clenched her teeth together and bit back the words that threatened to spill. Why couldn't Maira shut up? She began to regret letting Maira talk to her in the first place. She'd already known she was following because Kade had asked it of her. Why did she need it confirmed? Why did she always feel the need to ask questions? Amber held back a sigh.

"Silent treatment. Good call. It can be effective against a lot of people. Not me though. It just means I can talk without being interrupted." Maira grinned at Amber, laughing when there was no response. "I'd ask you if you were going to the party tonight, but I guess it'd be pointless since you wouldn't tell me anyway. I don't even know if you knew about it. We could take you with us if you want to go and haven't been invited. Jessica and Danielle are holding it. They're not related, don't even look alike, but you'd swear they were twins. It's the way they act and talk."

Amber walked a little faster. It didn't slow down Maira's words like she'd hoped.

"They didn't want to invite us, but Flinn made them. I'm not sure which one is his girlfriend, or even if any of them are. They hang around him like groupies. He doesn't seem to mind though. Kade hates it. I had to get rid of a couple of groupies that seemed to want to worship at his feet. I think it's in the blood. Something about the power of their ancestors is even noticed by you humans. The more popular the person the more they seem to be drawn to the two of them."

"Can't you shut up?" Amber stopped, rounding on Maira. "And quit grinning at me like that."

"How are you feeling after your run in with the wyvern this morning?"

"Just great."

Maira chuckled. "Are you always so sweet-natured or do I bring out the best in you?"

"Look. I'm not interested in talking. Or making

friends. As soon as I can I'm out of this town. I've got a life. One that I like. And I'm getting back to it as soon as I can." Maybe she'd make that her mantra. Got a life, like it, going back. Got a …

"Lives have a tendency not to wait on you."

"I don't want your little words of wisdom. Keep them for someone who cares." Amber started to walk again.

Maira walked silently beside Amber for nearly a minute before she spoke again. "So, where are we going?"

"How the hell would I know? I don't know anything about this town and I don't want to."

"So… what? Are you going to put your life on a shelf for the next few months and then pull it out again, dust it off and hope you haven't outgrown it?"

"Why bother getting to know anyone here? I won't see them again. Who's going to drive the nearly four hours it'd take to come and visit me?"

"I could probably be there in an hour with a tail wind."

"Really?" Amber stopped again and eagerly faced Maira. "Could you take me there?" She wanted to see Crystal face to face band demand answers.

Maira shook her head. "You'll have to ask Kade. He's stronger than I am. It'd take me a couple of hours to get there with a passenger. He could probably do it in an hour and a half."

"Why won't you take me?"

"Because that wasn't part of my orders."

"And you do everything Kade tells you to?"

"I try."

"That's…" Amber shook her head, at a loss for words. "How can you? How demeaning. It's as bad as slavery."

"You don't understand our society. My family is full of well-known warriors. Many have served under famous Gold Warriors. This is my last chance to serve a Gold Warrior."

"Is Kade famous?"

Maira shook her head. "No, but hopefully he will be one day."

"Why's it your last chance?"

Maira grinned wryly. "Apparently I have a major flaw."

"Only one?"

Maira laughed. "Only one that they've listed the past two times a Gold Warrior terminated my services. I have a slight problem with remembering to follow orders. If Kade decides I'm not suitable, that's it. No more chances. What is it you humans like to say? Three strikes, you're out."

"Why do you need warriors, anyway?"

"Why do you?"

"We don't."

"Yes you do. You call them soldiers."

"To protect our country. And to protect those who are weaker than us and are being attacked."

"Exactly."

"Huh?" Amber frowned, trying to make sense of Maira's words.

"There are millions of wyverns and sometimes they even attack in the thousands. Not to mention renegade dragons and those wanting more power than others. Just like in your world. And that's only the start of the list."

"But wouldn't we notice if there were thousands of wyverns in the one place?"

Maira shook her head. "This conversation is getting into territory that's becoming complicated. Do you know where we're headed yet?"

Amber stared at Maira as she tried to catch up with the conversation. "What time does the party start?" She was pleased to see it was Maira's turn to flounder.

"Any time after seven. Although it's probably not worth going until nine. Only the desperate will arrive at seven."

"Can you take off your bracelets?"

"Are you asking if I can physically remove them or if I will remove them?"

"My mum is strange about black jewellery."

Maira stared at her for a moment before she glanced around. The street was deserted. She pressed her left arm against her chest and covered it with her right hand. She ran it along the length of her arm and the bracelets disappeared. It looked like she slid them off and yet there were no bracelets left in her hand when she finished.

Amber blinked, staring at Maira's bare arms. "What the-"

"Scales. I reform them instead of completely changing. It was hard to maintain when I first started doing it. Not many of us can. Most of us can only be one or the other, not both at once."

Amber took a deep breath. "Help me talk my mother into letting me go to this party. I might as well go. Anything'd be better than staring at my bedroom walls." She strode towards her grandmother's home, ignoring the ache in her legs. The rest of the trip back was silent. She glared at Maira. Typical of her to be quiet when she needed a distraction.

Amber went straight to the kitchen and found it empty. Her note was still stuck under the magnet.

Taking it down, she shoved it in her pocket and went looking for her mother. She found her in the back downstairs room, which was a sewing room, or torture chamber, if her mother's expression was anything to go by.

"What a surprise. You don't show up when there's work to be done unless you have a buffer." Helen's gaze landed on Maira as she spoke the last word.

Amber tried hard to ignore her grandmother's words. They dug into her and made her want to deny the accusation. Instead, she turned to her mother and focused her attention on the person who'd say yes or no to the party. She glanced towards Maira. "This is Maira. She's in my Art class."

Donna rose from the sewing machine. "Nice to meet you, Maira."

Maira smiled slightly. "Thank you."

"Maira and her brothers are going to a party tonight and asked if I wanted to go too," Amber said.

"For someone who hated it here and wasn't interested in nothing or no one, you've changed your tune pretty quick," Helen said sharply.

Amber continued to watch her mother. She wouldn't let her grandmother bother her. She hoped. "You did say you wanted me to be more involved. Or was that just talk?"

Donna turned to Maira. "Will there be adult supervision at the party?"

Maira shook her head. "No. And Kade's my cousin, not brother. And Brann is no relative."

Amber shrugged. "Brother, cousin. He's still family. So can I go?"

"Well…"

"Look, Mum, don't take all day to decide or I'm going to change my mind again. I had planned to lock myself in my room, but Maira insists anyone not at the party will be considered not worth knowing."

"When will it finish?"

"Late. Which is why I thought I might stay at Maira's place."

"And is there adult supervision there?"

Maira shook her head again.

"I guess that means I'm hanging out in my room again. Thanks, Mum. I told her you wouldn't go for it. Glad to see I can rely on you to be consistent." Amber turned to leave.

"Don't try that reverse psychology on me. It won't work."

Amber shook her head. "I wouldn't think about it. I told Maira I'd only come if I could sleep over. It looks like I'll get out of having to go after all. Thanks."

"Are you going to let her get away with talking to you like that, Donna?" Helen demanded.

"Mum-" Donna began.

"Don't worry about it, Mum," Amber interrupted. "It's Hicksville. How exciting will a party be here? Half the people are probably inbred morons."

"You will stop calling my town Hicksville," Helen snapped.

Amber shrugged.

"Don't give me that attitude, miss. I don't go calling Brisbane Murderopolis."

Amber grinned. "Way to go, Grandma. I didn't know you had it in you. I actually quite like that name." She had no idea if it was accurate or not and didn't care if it was. All she cared was that it was her city and she wanted to return to it.

Helen turned to Maira who stood quietly watching the drama unfold before her. "I don't know what you see in my granddaughter."

"She's new to our school. I thought she'd be interested in making friends, but I'm beginning to wonder."

"Who's having the party?" Donna asked Maira.

"It's at Jessica Chambers' place."

Donna nodded and turned to Amber. "You'll ring

me and check in when you arrive, when you leave and when you get to Maira's house."

"You're letting me go?" Amber feigned surprise. Although she hadn't been completely certain her mother would let her go even with all the guilt she'd probably be feeling over tricking her into moving.

"You have got to be joking," Helen exclaimed.

Donna ignored her mother and continued to face Amber. "I grew up here. I know Jessica's mother. She was always quiet at school. I'll have all the details of the party by Monday afternoon. You might want to remember that."

"Just great. Small towns suck. I might as well stay home. It'll be as bad as having you there holding my hand."

"Come on, Amber. Why don't we go and see what you've got to wear?" Maira glanced between Amber and Donna.

Amber grunted, turning towards the doorway.

"Nice meeting you." Maira looked first to Donna and then Helen before she followed Amber.

"That girl is going to end up ruining her life and causing you nothing but heartache." Helen's words followed Amber out of the room.

She took the stairs two at a time, closing and

locking her bedroom door the moment Maira stepped inside. "Thanks."

"I'm not sure how I helped, or if I helped at all."

Amber grinned. "If I act too eager to go anywhere, she always thinks something is planned. So when I don't want to go, I act like I can't survive if I don't get to go and then sulk for a couple of days when she doesn't let me. My brother figured it out and told me in exchange for not dobbing on him when I caught him sneaking back in one morning."

"How odd. You humans are such strange creatures."

"Are you telling me dragons always say exactly what they mean?"

Maira grinned. "No, not at all. We have our politics, but our parents can't be so easily fooled."

"Can they read your mind or only talk in your mind?"

Maira laughed. "By the time we're teens they can't enter without permission. But then that's a dead give away at times. They also give us more freedom. They believe in survival of the fittest. I don't suppose it's easy for them, but if you want to make a place for yourself in our society, then you have certain... I guess you could call them rites of passage to pass.

Otherwise you could end up being ostracised and that's as good as a death sentence."

Amber stared at Maira, her words making her glad to be human. A death sentence for not fitting into society? "What do you get for murder?"

"Huh?"

"If one dragon kills another. What then?"

"It depends. If it's a renegade who has attacked you, then nothing. Okay, maybe congratulations. If you've attacked a dragon weaker than you, probably death if the family finds out. Our laws are different to yours. Survival of the fittest. Clans. Warrior ties. It's complicated."

"You… you get away with… murder?"

Maira shrugged. "Not exactly. And it isn't always murder. We still have battles to the death. If you invoke that right it's usually over something serious."

She had enough problems in her own life. She couldn't start taking on the problems of an entire society. She pushed the disquieting thoughts from her mind and strode over to her open wardrobe. "What sort of clothes will everyone be wearing?" When Maira didn't answer, Amber turned to face her.

Maira looked puzzled. "Clothes?"

"Yeah, what are you wearing to the party?"

Maira shook her head as she slowly walked over

to the wardrobe. "Clothes. Your mind jumps around like a cricket."

Amber frowned, tempted to argue that comment. It had been a perfectly logical question.

Chapter Seven

Amber sipped the drink in her hand as her gaze scanned the noisy, dimly lit room. It was crowded with people from school as well as others she didn't recognise. That didn't mean they weren't from her school, just that if they went, she hadn't noticed them or they didn't warrant her attention.

She sighed heavily and watched as Kade glanced her way before he turned back to talk to Maira and Brann. They were several metres from her and she wondered if he'd actually heard her sigh over the sound of talking and music or if it was a coincidence he'd turned towards her at that moment.

Her attention was caught by a boy walking towards her. He smiled when she looked at him. The last thing she wanted was to put up with someone trying to hook up with her. She looked him up and down and gave him her most disdainful expression before she turned slightly, her shoulder in his direction. She watched as Kade continued to talk to his companions. Or would 'warriors' be the correct term? Amber's lips smiled slightly. Maira and Brann looked as far from warriors as it was possible to be.

Brann had draped his arm around Maira's shoulders and his fingers lightly brushed back and forth. They wore black clothes and Maira had her usual jewellery, glinting and gleaming as her bare arms moved when she spoke. Her dress was long, the only concession she'd made to the cooler night and Amber believed it was made of the same leather as Brann and Kade's pants. The dress was probably warmer than needed with the press of bodies that kept the chill at bay.

"Hey."

Amber glanced at the boy who stood beside her. He was tall, blond and athletic looking. She made sure her expression showed how uninterested she was, mentally cursing Kade for deserting her within minutes of arriving. What was so important he'd had to take Maira and Brann aside? "Not interested."

"You don't know what I'm offering."

"Still not interested."

"I noticed you came with Kade. You're wasting your time there."

"My time to waste."

"And making friends with Maira won't help. Enough have tried that trick."

"Mind your own business."

He held out his hand. "Justin Chambers."

Amber ignored his hand. "You're related to Jessica?"

"Our parents tell me we're siblings, but I swear one of us was adopted." He grinned and lowered his hand.

"Why are you hassling me?"

"Because I'm not blind."

"How much?"

"What?"

"The bet. How much?"

"What bet?"

Amber let her gaze fall on the two boys who had watched Justin's progress, or lack of, talking and elbowing each other the entire time. "And what were the terms? Dance? Flirt back? Kiss? Go with you to your bedroom?"

"It wasn't like that."

Amber smiled, her eyes cold. "You wouldn't be the first, and you won't be the last. Your mistake was thinking you could goad me into spending time with you. I'm a master at that technique. Run back to your friends and pay up. I have better things to do with my time."

"Like what?"

Amber's smile became warm and she handed him her drink. Without answering, she turned and wove her way through the scattering of people between her and Kade. He looked up before she reached him, his gaze meeting hers.

"What are you planning?"

"I thought we weren't to use this method of talking?" She came to a stop in front of him, her smile still in place. Maira and Brann nodded towards her and, with a grin and wave from Maira, departed.

"We're shielded. I'm close enough to you it isn't difficult. Now, what are you up to?"

"I hope I didn't scare them away."

"Amber."

She grinned, placing her hands high on his chest. "Dance with me?" She took another step closer. There was only centimetres separating them.

Kade's eyes narrowed. "What are you trying to prove?"

"Nothing. Just sending out a message. Think of it as a way to repay me for all the problems you've caused me."

"Then we're even?"

"Nearly."

"Even."

Amber let her hands travel up to lock behind his neck, pulling his head closer. Her eyes closed as their lips met and her heartbeat raced. Time suspended and sounds receded. Kade's hands came to rest on her hips. Amber struggled to remember her plan. Then the fire in her veins turned to a crackle of energy in the air. She pulled back to stare up at Kade, a question in her eyes.

He didn't answer. He grasped one of her hands and pulled her through the crowd, headed for the front door. People stumbled out of his way, their gazes falling on Amber. She kept a smile hovering on her lips. She didn't know what was going on, but she wasn't about to let anyone else know. This would work out much better. She knew they all assumed he was desperate to get her alone. Let them think that. And if Justin didn't understand this message then he was blind as a bat.

Outside, Amber noticed Flinn striding down the street. Kade swore and moved quicker. As soon as they were out of earshot, Amber asked, "What's going on?"

Kade dropped her hand and started to unbutton his shirt. "I need to find somewhere to stash you. Somewhere safe."

"Why?" The crackle in the air made the hair on her arms sit up. "It's that Pliethin again, isn't it?"

"Yeah. I have to get to it before Flinn."

"Why?"

"Because there's only one here. I don't know how long it'll take to regenerate. Months at least."

"And then what? You go back to your people?"

Kade shook his head as he slipped his arms out of his shirt. "Take care of this for me."

Amber automatically took the shirt he pressed against her and then held it away from her when something made her stomach itchy. She brushed a couple of black hairs off her skin. "It's got cat hair on it."

"And?"

"It makes me itchy." She brushed at her clothes and arms, wishing she'd had time to collect her jacket before they'd left.

Kade grabbed it off her and threw it towards the base of a tree. "Guess that's another one lost."

Amber noticed several cat hairs on her arm and brushed them off. Luckily she'd left some space between her and Kade when they'd been kissing or it would have ruined her message to Justin. They hurried past the streetlight and back into the shadows.

"I'm not staying on my own. You try and leave me and I'll scream loud enough to hurt your mind."

"Amber–"

"No. You said you'd protect me. Then the first time that stupid energy thing appears you want to ditch me. Where are Brann and Maira? Why can't they stay with me?"

"I don't have time for this." Kade stopped and faced her, frustration colouring his voice.

"Then stop arguing and take me with you." She wrapped her arms around herself, trying to ignore the cold night air.

"I can't fly fast with you on my back. Not without you coming off."

"A saddle would be good. Can't you alter your appearance like the way Maira makes jewellery from her scales?"

"I wish," Kade muttered as he glanced around. He strode down the side of a house and became a dragon long enough to slice the rope from an empty clothesline. He knotted it into a harness, making a large loop at the top to carry it by. "Put your legs through this. And listen when I tell you something. No questions. No matter what I say."

"Aye, aye captain." Amber slid her legs through the harness.

"Do you want to be left behind?"

Amber stared at him for a moment, thinking of the wyvern. "Fine. I'll listen." Before she had time for any other words, Kade became a dragon and lifted the loop of the harness. She squealed when they were suddenly airborne, then laughed as she was dragged through the air, the wind rushing at her, causing her to shiver from the cold. Excitement burst through her and she grinned as she clung to each side of the loop that Kade held. She wanted to throw back her head and yell. But she guessed Kade would have something to say about that. Not exactly the way to avoid attention. Roller coasters were going to be extremely tame after this.

The ground rushed towards her. The crackle in the air pressed in on her. Ahead she could see Flinn. Two wyverns flew towards them. Fear mingled with the excitement. Kade slowed as a tree loomed in front of them.

"Stay in the tree." Kade deposited her in the branches and took off, flying straight towards the wyverns.

Amber tried to get comfortable, wrapping the loop around her waist so it didn't get caught on the branches. She was glad she'd chosen to wear long black pants with her short-sleeved shirt that left a few centimetres of skin showing at her waist. She wore her usual boots and guessed they'd make it near impossible to get out of the tree if she needed to.

She peered into the night and tried to see what was happening. Every now and then she saw a gleam as something caught the moonlight that peeked through streaky clouds. Every sound had her turning her head. Then a wyvern flew towards her with a dragon close behind it. For a moment she thought it was Kade, but the scales were dark blue rather than a golden brown. Flinn came in fast, flying above the wyvern. He headed straight for her. So did the wyvern. Neither seemed interested in her.

Amber looked up and saw a ball of light above her head. It seemed to be caught in the branches. She reached out to touch it.

"No!" She recognised Flinn's mental voice. It was the same as his verbal one.

"What's happening?" Kade came towards her from the right, having dealt with the other wyvern. *"Don't touch!"*

He was too late. Amber's hand closed over the Pliethin. A jolt of energy made her cry out. Losing her balance, she tumbled from the tree. Kade scooped her from mid air, his claws wrapped around her arm that held the Pliethin, causing pain to shoot through her shoulder. He slowed quickly as her feet hit the ground. Amber's knees buckled and Kade closed his arms around her as they sprawled across the ground, Kade human again. A jolt went through her and she screamed, continuing to lie dazed on the earth when he let go of her. She watched as Kade held the Pliethin while he transformed into a dragon.

She stared up at him as he blazed gold above her, his head thrown back. Flinn had vanished. The last wyvern came in from behind Kade. She didn't know why he hadn't already reached them.

Forcing herself to her feet, she tried to run, throwing one hand up protectively. "No!" A ball of flame flew from her hand towards the wyvern, barely missing Kade. Amber's knees gave out on her again and she kneeled on the ground, staring at her hand, fear exploding through her like the fireball had exploded against the wyvern. She looked at Kade who seemed oblivious to his surroundings, still a dragon and bathed in gold light from the Pliethin.

Amber struggled to her feet as the wyvern picked itself up off the ground. Its clawed wings flapped and its mouth opened. A screech tore through the air and Amber winced at the sound. She started to cover her ears with her hands then recalled the fireball she'd flung at the wyvern. She immediately dropped them.

The wyvern screeched again, streaking forward.

Amber held her hand up in the hope another fireball would erupt. Nothing. Panic rushed through her. She cursed Flinn for leaving. Kade, still a golden glow, had his head flung back, arms… claws… outstretched and his eyes closed. He gripped the Pliethin tight. No help there. And the wyvern wasn't interested in him anymore. Its red eyes gleamed as they focused on her. Amber turned and ran. She didn't know if the fireball was a one-off, a fluke or even a hallucination. It didn't matter. She couldn't do it at will and she didn't have the time to stand there and figure out how. Dodging behind a tree, she considered calling out mentally to Kade, but didn't know if he should be interrupted. Would that harm him? Harm her?

She dodged to the other side of the tree as the wyvern came around, its serpent like tail flicking like an irate cat. It ended in a barb and Amber forced her gaze away from it. Focusing on the damage that tail could cause wouldn't help her think clearly.

When the wyvern came around the tree again, Amber sprinted into the open, forcing her legs to go faster. She tried to see the ground she ran across, but it was full of shadows. Stumbling in a hole, she sprawled face first onto the ground, rolling to her back before she came to a stop. The wyvern, claws outstretched, came straight at her.

Fear exploded in her as she threw up her hands in an automatic gesture of protection. Fire rushed at the wyvern. A smell like burnt hair filled the air. Amber coughed. The wyvern screeched. Its wings pumped strongly, causing a downdraft that swirled the dirt around Amber and made her close her eyes, coughing as the dust irritated her throat. She sat up when the air settled and watched the wyvern fly away.

She forced her shaking limbs to obey her and stood, staggering over to Kade to drop onto the ground in front of him. Feeling tears burn her eyes, she forced them away. She hated weepy people. No matter the circumstances. As she watched, the glow around Kade faded and he dropped to the ground, human again. He looked as exhausted as she felt. Exhausted and dazed.

Kade stared at the Pliethin in his hand. It no longer seemed like a ball of energy. It was dull, grey, misshapen. "Thank you. I'm sorry it was necessary." He opened his hand and the creature hovered above his palm and then faded.

"Is it dead?"

Kade slowly shook his head. His voice was equally slow. "When it's not in physical contact with this world it can fade to another."

"Another world?"

Kade looked around. "Where's Flinn?"

"He flew off. I'm guessing it was the moment you had the Pliethin, but I'm not entirely sure since I'd just hit the ground."

"The wyvern?"

"He left it here."

Kade swore, reaching for her. Still sitting in the dirt, Amber pulled back out of his reach. "He flew off and left the wyvern here?"

She nodded.

"He didn't deal with it first?"

Amber shook her head. She dreaded the question she knew would come.

"What happened to the wyvern?"

Answers floated around in Amber's mind. *I'm as much a freak as you now. I tried to barbeque it. It didn't like the taste of me so it took off.* She discarded all of them and shrugged.

"What are you hiding?" Kade grabbed her wrist when she tried to move away from him again. His grip tightened when she pulled back. Kade closed his eyes.

Amber felt the invasion of her mind immediately. She resisted, angry that he would force her to tell him what had happened. She focused on him. Filled her mind with the image of him sitting in front of her, eyes closed, arm stretched out. She raised her hand so she could add that to the image.

He retreated. "Amber, you have to tell me."

She chose option B. "I tried to barbeque him."

"You did what?"

Amber opened her fist, palm up, and held her other hand near it. "Fire." She stared at her palms. "I threw fire at it."

Chapter Eight

Kade's grip loosened and he placed his free hand against her other palm. "Fire?" His word was a whisper.

Amber didn't answer. Instead she watched their two hands that were pressed together. Heat generated between them. She gasped when fire bloomed in her hand as Kade took his away. Fire clung to his palm. She could feel the heat against her own palm, but her hand remained unchanged. A flickering ball of fire rested in her palm and it didn't even raise the slightest blister on her skin.

Kade swore and snapped his hand closed. The fire went out. Amber mimicked him, dousing the fire in her own palm.

"The Pliethin." Kade stared at her hands.

"Is that it? Is that all it did?" When Kade watched her cautiously, Amber rose to her knees and slammed her hands against his chest, breaking from his grip in the process. "Tell me that's all it did. The last thing I want to be is a freak like you and your warriors." Option A after all. Amber shut her eyes at the flicker of hurt that crossed Kade's face. She opened her eyes again. His expression was closed. "Okay, so I thought it was kind of cool when it wasn't me. I don't want this. I'm an ordinary person, with an ordinary life. I like that. You start being extraordinary and people expect more of you."

"No one will know of this. Do you hear me? No one."

"I don't want it. Tell me how to get rid of it. Will it wear off with your blood?" Kade's sudden inability to meet her gaze alarmed her. "This is because of your blood, isn't it?"

Kade nodded. "I think so. Amber…" he cleared his throat. "I haven't heard of this happening before."

"What do you mean?"

"The Pliethin. They affect only Gold Warriors. They don't cause any change in other dragons. Many have tried. Nothing has happened. Only Gold Warriors, and the effects on them are permanent."

"Have they tried when they have the blood of a Gold Warrior in them?"

Kade nodded. "It doesn't work on those that aren't Gold."

"So you don't know if this is permanent?" Silence met her question. "Answer me!"

"I'm sorry, Amber. I screwed up in a major way."

"No!"

"Amber–"

"No!" She struggled to her feet. Anger burned away exhaustion.

Kade was beside her in seconds. "Let me take you to my house before you collapse."

She turned to face him. "My grandmother's."

"You don't want that."

"Don't tell me what I want!" She stopped abruptly as an image of her appeared in her mind. Someone wild, hair tangled, eyes blazing, teeth bared as she yelled. Dust coated her, leaves and twigs caught in the knots her hair had become. "I don't look like that."

"Let me take you to my home. Get cleaned up and we'll talk about you going to your home."

"It's my grandmother's home," Amber muttered. She stubbornly stared at Kade who only shrugged. "Fine. I'll get cleaned up and then you take me home." She unwrapped the loop of the harness from her waist. "You didn't tell me where Brann and Maira are."

"No. I didn't." He shimmered into dragon form, grabbed the loop and pulled her into the air with him.

Amber was too agitated to enjoy the flight to Kade's home. She had a glimpse of open paddocks for a moment before they landed in front of an old house with a verandah wrapped around two sides. They stepped in the front door and Amber paused to look around the lounge room, lit by the soft light of a floor lamp in the corner.

A lounge suite dominated the room, its floral fabric faded and worn in places. A television sat on one wall, DVDs and CDs scattered on the low cabinet it sat on. The floors were worn timber, no shine like those in her grandmother's house, and a rug lay on the floor in front of the lounge suite.

"Maira brought your bag over earlier." Kade gestured towards the overnight bag Amber had packed that afternoon.

She stared at it by the door. A lot had happened since then. Her whole life had been shattered. And to think she'd been upset about moving and starting a new school. At least she'd known what to expect. Now... now she didn't have a clue.

"Amber?"

"Where's the bathroom?" She picked up her bag.

Kade stared at her for a moment before he headed

for the only other door in the room. They stepped through a dark hallway and straight into a kitchen. Kade turned the light on and strode past the table that sat in the middle of the room, eight chairs around it, and to another doorway opposite the one they'd entered. A laundry ran along the back of the house. He gestured to the door on his left. She caught glimpses of shadowy trees and stars through the timber-framed windows that marched along the rear wall of the laundry.

"Towels are in the linen cupboard in the bathroom. I'll be in the kitchen when you're finished."

Amber didn't bother to answer him. She stepped inside the bathroom and carefully shut and locked the door, resisting the urge to slam it. She dropped her bag on the floor, grabbed a towel from the cupboard, shoved the towels that were already on the rack to the side and hung hers over the rack. Stripping off her clothes, she grimaced at the dust that floated around her and to the ground, frowning when she noticed a couple of cat hairs where the top of her pants had ended. Normally a red rash would have appeared with how long they'd been there. Maybe she was growing out of her allergy.

Another thought occurred to her as she stepped under the warm water of the shower head which was set over a claw foot bathtub. Maybe the Pliethin had cured her of her cat allergy. Yet another thing she could have lived without in favour of her life staying the same. She hated change. She knew people who thrived on it. She wasn't one of them.

Grabbing a bottle of shampoo that hung in a metal rack from the shower head, she wrinkled her nose. Orange blossoms. Now she'd smell like a garden. Just great. She guessed Maira owned it. The only other bottle was conditioner. Amber wondered what Brann and Kade used. Surely not orange blossoms. Her other choice was a cake of soap. Orange blossoms would have to do. She preferred berries.

By the time she finished in the bathroom, Amber felt more human. Or as human as it was possible to be when you could hold fire in your hands. Shuddering as she recalled the sensation, she wiped her hands against the long sleeved, short cotton dress she planned to wear to bed. She could still feel the heat in her hands.

As she stepped out of the bathroom, Kade came to the kitchen doorway. "You might as well throw your clothes in the washing machine."

Amber gathered up her dirty clothes, holding them away from her body, taking her phone from her pocket before she dumped them in the machine.

While she washed her hands at the laundry tub, Kade added washing powder and softener before he turned it on. Still remaining silent, Amber moved away from him to the back door. She opened it, surprised it wasn't locked, then remembered the front door hadn't been either. Dialling her mother's mobile number, she waited for her to answer.

"I was beginning to wonder when you were going to call it a night."

"Sorry, Mum. I forgot to ring you before we left. I'm already at Maira's house."

"Did you have a good time?"

Yeah, I was nearly eaten by a wyvern. She could just imagine what her mother would say if she said that. "I didn't know anyone there."

"Amber–"

"It was a waste of time." But now I can throw fireballs. Yet something else she was going to have to keep from her mother.

Donna sighed heavily. "Well, don't stay up all night talking. You know how cranky you get when you don't have enough sleep."

She doubted that would have been what her mother would have said if she'd told the truth. "Yeah, sure. I'll be home some time tomorrow afternoon."

"Ring me when you wake up."

"Don't go ringing me early to check on me. I'm not getting up before lunch."

There was silence for a moment. "If you'd give this place a chance-"

She'd done that and look where it had got her. "Night, Mum."

Another sigh. "Goodnight, Amber."

Amber left her phone on the bench top of the cupboards that ran from the door to the laundry tub and stepped into the cool night air. She crossed her arms, wishing she had her jacket.

"Will you be right while I have a shower?"

Amber ignored Kade, listening as he moved towards the bathroom, after a moment, and closed the door. She stepped further into the yard. Large trees were scattered around creating deeper shadows. Breathing in, a scent caught her attention.

Her head came up and her eyes narrowed. Anticipation raced through her and she slowly stalked forward, her feet sure and quiet. Her muscles tightened and she forced herself to keep moving slowly. The wind teased her with the scent and her mouth watered. Ever closer she came to the tantalising aroma. The shadows seemed to give up their secrets, lightening as if the moon had come out of hiding. She didn't bother to glance up and see, all her senses were focused on one thing. Then she saw him.

Head down, nibbling on the grass, the reddish brown coat sleek, the antlers rising from his head that suddenly lifted. He tensed, his head moved. Then he relaxed and went back to grazing. Amber, who had frozen at his movement, began to inch forward again. The stag continued to remain unaware.

"Amber!"

The stag leapt forward, tail up. Amber swore. She rounded on Kade to yell at him for scaring off her meal. Her jaw dropped as she realised exactly what she'd been thinking. Her hands came up to cover her mouth. "Oh my god! Oh no! Please no." Her voice trailed off to a whisper.

Kade reached her side in seconds, draping an arm around her shoulders. "What's wrong? Talk to me."

Amber could only shake her head, trying to understand what had happened. She let Kade guide her inside, dropping onto the kitchen chair he pulled out for her.

"Do you want a drink? Something to eat?"

Amber shook her head. Her eyes widened as her stomach did somersaults. Clapping a hand to her mouth, she focused on breathing. She wasn't going to throw up. And she wasn't going to think about the stag.

"Amber…"

Holding up her hand, she shook her head, still unable to speak. She dropped her head onto the table and waited for her stomach to settle. As soon as it had, she looked up at Kade who hovered beside her. "I was stalking that stag. I wanted to eat him." Hysteria bubbled up and she forced it down. It tinged her last words.

Kade dropped into the chair beside her. "Stalk?"

Amber nodded. "I could smell him. I didn't even think. Just reacted. I felt like I could tear him apart with my bare hands. Tell me I'm not going mad."

"Stalk."

"Will you stop saying that?" Amber hit the table with her open hand.

"What animal?"

"Stag."

"No, what animal did you remind yourself of?"

"I don't know. Pounce! I was tensed to pounce. A cat. A large cat. Tiger, panther, jaguar. Something like that."

Kade swore. He pushed away from the table and paced.

Amber stepped in front of him, her chair nearly

falling with how quickly she rose. "What's happening? Tell me!" She grabbed his upper arms.

"Panther."

"How do you know?"

"Those cat hairs?" When Amber nodded, Kade glanced away. "It wasn't Maira's pet. It was a panther."

"What!"

"They're returning it. Flinn thought it'd make a good meal. Maira argued with him about it. She won."

"You had panther hairs on your shirt?"

Kade nodded. "I'm sorry-"

"You stupid-" her fist aimed for his jaw.

Kade moved out of the way, catching her hand. "Enough! It wasn't deliberate. You were told to follow orders."

"Follow orders! I had Flinn and a wyvern coming straight for me. It was instinct to grab the Pliethin. I was scared out of my mind. I was stuck in a tree with a red-eyed beast whose claws were ready to tear me apart. I don't know what I was thinking. Or even if I was capable of thinking. I know I had a fleeting thought that I was going to die. But that might have been later. It's all a muddle. Tell me what this means."

"I don't know! Why do you think I'm suddenly

going to have the answers to this when I keep telling you I wouldn't have a clue? You can't tell anyone about this. Do you understand? No one. Especially not Flinn."

"Why?"

"Because he'll kill you if he thinks you're a threat to our people. I was going to bunk in Maira and Brann's room and let you have mine. But not now. I don't know when Flinn and his warriors will be home, but I won't leave you alone. He'll know something happened."

"And how could he know that?"

"He flew off and left the wyvern there to kill us. Any Gold Warrior who holds a Pliethin is not aware of their surroundings. At all. We shouldn't have survived the wyvern attack. You have to tell him you kept the wyvern occupied until I was myself again. That you kept running and dodging like you did the first time."

"He wanted us to die?" Her words were little more than a whisper. They echoed in her mind.

"We believe in survival of the fittest. I should have had Maira and Brann with me, but I didn't think Flinn would desert us like that. I shouldn't have let Maira get squeamish over a panther. Flinn had his people with him."

"I didn't see any other dragons."

"They were there. Keeping their distance, but ready in case they were needed."

"Where are they now?"

Kade shrugged. "I don't know. Probably with Flinn. And before you ask, I don't know where he is either."

Amber turned away. Exhaustion washed over her. "This is all such a mess."

"I'm sorry."

"Yeah, sure you are. But only because you're worried about what your old people will say."

Kade laughed softly. "Elders. And they're not all old. Well, not in the dragon sense. It's their title."

"Oh, who cares?" She turned abruptly so she could face him. She wanted to stop thinking about all this. "Where am I sleeping?"

"My room." He stepped back into the hallway and this time turned to his right. There were two doors at the end, one ahead, one on the right. Kade opened the door in front of him, turning on the light. He stepped out of the way so Amber could enter.

She stared at the king-sized bed before she turned to face Kade. "You better not be expecting me to share that with you."

"You mean to tell me that wasn't what you were

angling for earlier tonight?" When Amber only glared at him, Kade laughed and gestured towards the bed. "Don't worry, you'll be the only human in it tonight."

Was she still human? She didn't know. She took a hesitant step towards the bed, sending a cautious glance towards Kade. When he remained by the doorway, she threw back the covers and dropped onto the bed. "You can turn the light out now."

Kade rested his hand on the switch. "No invading my thoughts in your dreams." He smiled, turning out the light.

She blinked at the sudden darkness. When she blinked again she was surprised to find the room wasn't as dark as she'd first thought. She searched for the source of light. There was none. Rolling over so her back was to the door, she quickly closed her eyes, not wanting to think what it meant. But she couldn't help the thought, 'cats see in the dark', from invading her mind. Squashing it, she focused instead on reconstructing her own room, in her own home, in her mind. She wished she was there right now. Her grandmother's house would never be home.

Chapter Nine

Amber's eyes opened and she glanced around. Nothing. Whatever sound had woken her had stopped. She rolled onto her back and sat up. She was completely silent. Her movements didn't disturb the dragon curled on the bed with her, taking up most of the space. She felt like pushing him onto the floor. No other human! Swinging her legs over the side of the bed, she stood up, quietly crossing the room and letting herself out. Closing the door behind her, she wandered to the bathroom, returning to the kitchen once she'd finished in there.

Noise caught her attention and she stepped back into the laundry. Movement at the window drew her forward. Her eyes narrowed and she saw a bird jump from branch to branch in one of the trees outside. She could see each feather, the eyes that checked for danger and the way its head turned towards each sound. Easing the back door open, she stalked towards the tree. She leapt and grabbed one of the lower branches, swinging herself up. She paused. When the bird remained unaware of her, she pulled herself higher.

Crouching on the branch, she waited. The bird came near. It darted away. Closer. It paused to trill. Then it landed near her. Amber leapt up onto the next branch and her hand streaked out, grabbing the bird as it tried to fly away. She could feel its heart beat fast as it tried to struggle out of her grip. She could smell it. The tantalising smell of her prey filled her senses.

"Amber! What are you doing up there?"

Startled by Maira's words, Amber nearly fell from the tree, opening her hand to grab a branch. The bird darted away. She looked around, half dazed. Closing her eyes, she took a deep breath. "Trying to see how quickly I can be committed." She shakily descended the tree. Twice she almost fell.

"Committed to what?"

Flinn stepped out the back door. "What's she doing here?"

"I invited her. It's not like I can invite other females over. Not without a lot of preparation and planning and making sure everything looks normal. Do you think I enjoy being stuck in a house full of males all the time? Five to one are pretty bad odds."

"Then keep her out of my way." Flinn spun, striding back inside.

"Isn't he cheerful." Amber strode towards Maira. "Why did you tell him I'm here to even up the odds?"

"I didn't." Maira grinned. "Not once did I actually come out and say that. What he chooses to take from my words is his business."

Amber shook her head. "What have you got for breakfast?" She glanced in the direction the bird had flown, forcing herself not to think about it. Although today her stomach didn't rebel at the thought of eating a live animal. Horror rushed through her and she missed Maira's words. "Do you have breakfast cereal and milk?" When Maira looked at her in concern, she demanded, "What?"

"I said we often catch our own. There might be some bread in the fridge for when I make sandwiches for school lunches."

Kade appeared in the doorway, wearing only leather pants. "I wondered where you'd got to."

"Trying to catch a bird." Amber glared at Kade.

He laughed. When Maira opened her mouth to ask a question, he waved her away. She went without comment. "Walk with me." He dropped an arm around her shoulder, guiding her away from the house.

Wanting to talk to him, Amber remained at his side. "How do I stop this? I can't get up and leave the classroom when I notice prey outside."

"Maybe you need to take a few days off while you sort it out."

Amber pulled away from him. "Sort it out! And how the hell am I meant to do that? I wish I'd never met you." She spun away, striding towards the gum trees that stood on the other side of the open paddock they were in.

"Amber!"

She ignored Kade, breaking into a run when she heard him follow. He came closer. She could hear him. Smell him. He smelled like a predator. She ran faster, a long easy stride without effort. He ran beside her. She forced herself to move faster. Suddenly she loped across the ground, the grass rising up around her body, her paws silent. A rumble started in the back of her throat. She roared as she turned to face Kade. He stopped abruptly. Amber's eyes narrowed as she watched him. He took a step back.

He smelled like a predator, acted like prey. She sprung, powerful limbs throwing her forward. He shot off the ground, a dragon taking flight.

"Amber! You're human. Remember you're human."

Amber howled in rage as she looked up at him. An image pushed into her mind. Herself prowling back and forth, a panther with tattered cotton flapping around her. Shock shuddered through her. She felt herself change. It was like a shiver going through her body. Kade landed in front of her, human the moment he touched the earth. Amber rose from the ground, trying to pull the tatters of her dress around her, very few of the seams still intact.

"Maira's bringing you something to wear."

"I don't want this. Please. There has to be some way to make it go away."

"Amber, I'm-"

"If you say you're sorry, I'm going to turn into a panther and rip your limbs from your body."

Kade grinned. "Do you think you can turn into a panther at will?"

She glared at Kade, wanting to tell him she could change whenever she wanted, but she knew that wasn't true. She didn't have a clue how to change. Or how to throw fireballs. Or even what other surprises she had to look forward to. She stopped that train of thought immediately. What did it matter? She didn't want to be able to do any of those things. She wanted her life back. Unchanged. There had to be a way to fix this.

"Heads up."

At Maira's warning, Amber looked up. As soon as she did, the black and silver dragon dropped the clothes she carried, wheeled in the sky and flew towards the house. Amber caught the black leather, turned her back to Kade and quickly pulled on the long pants. Removing the tattered clothes, she slipped on the leather vest. Once she'd done up the buttons of the vest, she frowned when she notice the vest gaped a little. Maira filled it much better than she did.

She turned back to face Kade. "I want my clothes."

"Sure, if you don't mind ending up naked every time you shapeshift."

"Why don't these become tatters? Or even look like clothes when you become a dragon? They're made of the same material as your pants, aren't they?" She gestured towards his legs.

Kade nodded. "Yeah, they are. It's because they're dragon skin."

"It's-" Amber shook her head. Surely she'd misheard. "What?"

"Dragon skin. Don't worry, you're not wearing the skin of my family." He grinned. "Renegades. At least they become useful in death."

Amber opened her mouth to speak. Closing her mouth when words wouldn't form, she turned away. Her eyes closed as she tried to gather scattered thoughts. Just like cowhide, she tried to tell herself. Except cows didn't become human and hold conversations with you. She wore the skin of a dead person. Her eyes flew open. She had to get them off. Her fingers fumbled with the buttons. She pushed Kade away when he stepped in front of her, trying to grab her hands.

"No! Leave me be. I can't wear this."

"Amber–"

"No!"

"Don't be stupid."

"Stupid! Don't–"

"Stop it!" He captured her hands. "You're becoming hysterical. I think I liked you better as a panther."

"Let go of me." Her voice dropped, her teeth clenched together. She stared at him. Anger filled her.

"Amber, be realistic."

"Don't tell me what to do. I'm not one of your warriors. Leave me alone. I'm going back to my grandmother's and I never want to see you again. You talk to me at school and I'll pretend you don't exist." She didn't try to pull her hands away. She waited. Anger coursed through her body like energy waiting to be used. She held it in check. What the emotion might unleash terrified her. Fear had brought fireballs. Hunger called forth a panther. She didn't need any more complications.

"I'll have Brann make you a vest that fits better. And Maira can give you a pair of her leather shorts to wear under your school uniform."

"I'm not wearing the same clothes every day."

"I'll organise several for you. Any preference to colour or will black do?"

Amber's lips tightened. What choice did she have? Ending up naked in front of an entire school would have to be one of the worst things possible. Nearly as lethal as being hunted by a wyvern since she'd probably die of embarrassment. Her lips curved into a mocking smile. "The colour of your skin."

Kade laughed. "Light brown it is then."

The smile evaporated when Kade didn't take offence at her comment. "I want to go."

"I won't tell you I'm sorry since you don't want to hear that, but if you can think of anything I can do to make this easier for you, tell me."

Amber almost said there was nothing he could do. Yesterday's conversation with Maira came to mind. "I want you to take me home."

Kade nodded. "I know. You've already asked, but if-"

"No. My home. Not my grandmother's home. I want you to fly me there. Maira said you could do it in about ninety minutes."

"How long does it take to drive there?"

"Nearly four hours."

"And that would make this easier for you?" Kade looked sceptical.

Amber nodded. "I need to see someone."

"You can't tell them what's happened."

Amber shook her head. "I don't want to." Maybe if Crystal hadn't dropped out of her life she would have wanted to, but now she only wanted to find out exactly what had happened. "I just need to see them."

"When?"

"Now?"

Kade shook his head. "It needs to be after dark. I don't think you could manage the altitude I'd need to fly at in daylight to remain unseen."

"I'll be ready and waiting for you at quarter past five." Amber didn't wait for an answer. Pulling her hands away from his relaxed ones, she strode towards the house, amazed at how far she'd run. She wasn't a runner. She hated running. Well, she had, in her old life.

She considered running back to the house, wanting to get away from Kade who walked silently at her side. But it wasn't a good idea. Her stomach rumbled with hunger and she forced herself not to be distracted by the many warm bodies she could smell around her. Running might cause her to change and go hunting. That was the last thing she needed.

Maira waited at the back door for them. "I put your clothes in the dryer last night." She gestured towards the folded clothes on the bench near Amber's mobile phone and bag.

Amber nodded, gathered her gear and strode towards the bedroom. She wasn't going to wear the leather clothes home. That'd cause a million questions she couldn't answer. A light tap on the bedroom door just after she shut it had her glaring at it.

"Amber, I don't know what you plan to wear today, but I've got a pair of shorts here you might prefer." Maira tapped on the door again when Amber remained silent.

Amber finally opened the door and took the shorts. She tried to close the door, but Maira put her foot against the base. She was tempted to tell her to leave her alone. But she already knew how well Maira listened to what she thought when it went against her orders. Instead, she stared at a point past Maira's shoulder.

"When you've got the shorts on, give me a yell. You need to be measured for your own clothes." Maira moved her foot.

Amber locked the door as soon as she closed it and pulled off the long pants to replace them with the shorts. She stared at the door. A sigh escaped. Maira wouldn't be put off. She might as well give in and at least appear to be choosing to be measured rather than forced. Swinging the door open, she was startled to see both Brann and Maira. When she stepped back, they entered the room. Brann held a dressmaker's tape measure.

Having her waist measured was bearable. Hip to ankle wasn't too bad. When Brann tried to measure her inner leg, she stepped back.

"Stay still," Brann muttered as he tried to measure her again.

"Problem?" Kade asked from the doorway.

Amber's head snapped up. She wondered how long Kade had been there. "Not at all."

Kade smiled. "Sure?"

Amber glared at him while Brann continued to measure her. When he measured her chest, her glare intensified. Brann stepped back to scribble the last measurement in his notebook and Amber went to her bag she'd dropped on the bed. Even though the nights were cool, the days were still warm. So she'd brought a short-sleeved dress to wear.

Pulling the dress from her bag, she turned to her audience. "If you don't mind?" She shook the dress to let them know what she meant.

"I'll meet you out the front." Kade started to turn away.

"You're not driving me home."

"Maira's had hardly any sleep." Kade stepped into the room.

"Mum would freak if I returned with you when I left with Maira."

"I'll manage." Maira leaned against Brann who put his arm around her waist.

Amber hesitated. Maira did look tired. But she didn't want the drama that would erupt if Kade took her home.

"We'll all go. I'll drive." Kade turned and walked from the room. Decision made.

Amber glared after him, wishing she could throw something at his retreating back. He glanced down the hallway towards her as he entered the lounge room and stepped out of her vision. Brann and Maira followed his example. Amber closed the door behind them, leaning against it. It was an effort to stay focused. She needed to eat. And soon. Her ears pricked as she heard a movement in the ceiling. Her nose twitched. Possum! She pushed away from the door and moved stealthily across the floor as she sniffed it out.

She swore as she realised what she was doing. There had to be a way to get rid of this. She couldn't very well go hunting when she was at school tomorrow. She hurriedly dressed, grabbed her things and went outside to the front verandah. She didn't want to be alone. That was when it was worse. It was easy to lose herself when there was no one around to remind her she was human. And she was human. She had to be.

As soon as she was in the front seat of the car, she sent a text to let her mother know she was on the way. She didn't think she could speak to her. She needed to calm herself first. Although she had no idea how she was going to manage that.

The drive was quiet. Maira fell asleep in the backseat, her head against Brann's shoulder. Amber kept her gaze mostly ahead after the single glance behind. When they pulled up in front of her grandmother's house, she jumped out. They followed. She'd hoped they'd get the message and drive off. Amber looked at each of them. Maira yawned.

They each wore the same long leather pants. Maira had put a blouse on over her vest. Brann and Kade wore light, long sleeved shirts. Brann maroon, Kade a green dark enough to almost be black. None of them smiled. There was a slight air of menace about them. Amber had serious misgivings about inviting them inside. Kade grinned and his whole demeanour seemed to change. Charismatic, everyone's best friend. She forced herself not to answer his smile with one of her own. If he weren't so gorgeous it'd be much easier to stay angry with him. She turned to open the front door.

Her mother and grandmother were in the sewing room again. She guessed it was again and not still. The image of her grandmother keeping her mother working at the sewing machine all night caused a fleeting smile.

"I'm home." Amber knew she stated the obvious. But neither of them had looked up at her entrance. They did now. She pointed to each of her companions in turn. "You've met Maira. That's her cousin Kade and that's Brann." Amber didn't know whether to be annoyed or relieved when Donna and Helen returned the smiles aimed at them.

Kade stepped forward, holding out his hand to Helen. "Nice to meet you." He took Donna's hand once Helen released him. His smile didn't falter.

Donna glanced at her watch. "No wonder I'm getting hungry. It's after midday. Have you kids eaten yet? Do you want to stay for lunch?"

"Thanks, but we've got plans for this afternoon. We just wanted to come in and say hello first," Kade said.

"I'm hungry." Amber worried her mother wouldn't bother to make lunch for her either. When Donna nodded, she said, "I'll see them out to their car."

Amber closed the front door behind her so their words wouldn't drift inside. She stepped close to Kade. "You better not be late."

"Make sure your doors are unlocked." Kade strode to the car. Maira and Brann followed.

Amber watched Kade drive away. A small part of her wished she was in the car with them. The part that wasn't looking forward to the interrogation she'd have to endure from her mother. She frantically planned out what she'd say about the party as she walked back to the kitchen, trying to ignore the urge to hunt down the dog she could smell nearby.

Chapter Ten

Amber rose to her feet, then sat on the bed again. She was meant to be asleep with a headache. If she started to pace, her mother would knock on the door and demand to know what was wrong. She wore long leather pants and a light jacket over a matching vest. She'd debated wearing her boots. They were her favourite ones and had taken her months to save for. She didn't want them to end up in tatters. They were all she had to wear, except the school shoes her mother had bought.

She frowned as she thought of the ugly uniform she'd have to wear the next week. She'd liked being able to wear normal clothes to school while she'd waited for her size to come in. Someone had bought the last few uniforms in her size a couple of days before she'd arrived. It was good being an average size at times like that.

Her head came up as the scents around her changed. Rising to her feet, she quietly crossed the room. The French doors opened before she reached them. Kade remained in the doorway, waiting for her. He wore a leather vest with his long pants and held out the jacket she'd left behind at the party. His gaze dropped to her feet.

"Guess we'll have to get you a pair of boots so you don't ruin those ones."

"I like mine." Amber wanted to take back the words the moment she'd spoken them. She did like hers. And she didn't want them wrecked. She took her jacket from him and tossed it on the bed.

Kade shrugged. "Are you ready to go?" At Amber's nod, Kade loosened one of the two belts at his waist and slid it up to sit under his arms. "When I change, this metal loop the belt threads through will be embedded in my scales so you can clip yourself to it." He spun the belt so the loop was on his back. "It's made from a metal that won't change with me." He undid the other belt he wore. It had a clip on the end of the long leather. "For you to wear. Dragon-leather in case you change."

Amber had made sure she'd eaten before retiring to her room. She wasn't going to change, not if she had anything to say about it. As soon as her belt was on, Kade stepped onto the balcony.

"This might be a little difficult. I can't perch on the rails for long. Maybe you should hop on my back and hook yourself on before I change."

Amber looked over the rail to the ground. She turned to face Kade, who had a slight smile, and forced back the fear. She didn't want to throw fireballs at anything. Ever. She eyed his broad shoulders and his muscular arms, hoping he wouldn't drop her when he changed shape. "Okay."

Kade squatted so Amber could hook herself to the metal loop and wrap her arms and legs about him. He stood up. "Hold me lightly. I change quickly."

Amber had no sooner loosened her grip then he seemed to jump, change in midair and soar into the sky almost instantaneously. Her arms felt like they exploded with scales that scraped against her body as she struggled to stay on. The leather belt tightened on her waist, but held. Kade levelled out and Amber's struggle to hold on ceased. She breathed deeply when she realised she held her breath. Forcing herself to remain calm, she focused on her breathing, closing her eyes. She would not change. She'd stay even-tempered and control those traits that made her a freak.

Partway through the journey, Amber began to grow bored. She'd sat up earlier, only her legs wrapped around him. Now she leaned forward, arms flung around Kade and her body pressed against his back, closing her eyes to rest. She didn't plan to sleep. Not while they flew at a life ending height above ground. Her body had different plans.

She was jarred awake as Kade landed in a well-treed park. Opening her eyes, she blinked. The thick shadows receded and she searched the area, trying to figure out where they were.

"Hold on. I'm going to change."

Amber nearly ended up on the ground when Kade became human. She clung tighter, her legs wrapped around his waist. He knelt and she let go, standing shakily once she unhooked herself. Wrapping the tail of the belt around her waist, she hooked it on the metal loop that was used instead of a buckle. Kade faced her as he returned his belt to his waist and tightened it.

"Shall we find a taxi?"

Amber shook her head. "I don't have that much money on me."

Kade shrugged. "I have. Come on."

They found a taxi and Amber gave Crystal's address. When they were nearly there she began to worry Crystal might be out. Although after seven on a Sunday night, her parents usually expected her to be in her room doing homework. The taxi pulled up in front of Crystal's home and Amber hopped out while Kade paid.

"A dragon with a credit card?" Amber looked up at Kade as he came to stand beside her. The taxi pulled out onto the road, driving away.

Kade grinned. "The modern equivalent of a hoard. You still can't beat the feel of gold and jewels though."

Amber automatically returned his smile. "I guess not." She frowned when she looked over at Crystal's house. A deep breath and then she headed for the side gate. Kade followed silently. Amber made her way to Crystal's window, thankful of her new ability to walk without noise as she passed the lounge room where Crystal's parents watched the television. She stopped at Crystal's window, staring at the light seeping out around the drawn curtain, worried about what Crystal might tell her.

"Do you want me to stay with you or disappear?"

It took Amber a minute to decide. "Disappear." When Kade stepped back into the deeper shadows, she tapped lightly on Crystal's window. Then she tapped a little harder.

The curtain was drawn back and Crystal stared at her. She quickly opened the window and pulled the screen out. Throwing her leg over the sill, she clambered outside to stand in front of Amber. The two of them walked quietly to the garden seat hidden at the rear of the yard under a green arbour.

The familiarity of it startled Amber. How many times had she tapped on Crystal's window so they could sit on the garden seat and chat when they were meant to be elsewhere. Like in bed asleep. But it was different. This time lacked the easy flow of words.

Crystal clasped her hands tightly in her lap, staring down at them. "I couldn't tell you sorry. I was stupid. That wasn't forgivable."

"Why?"

"It started as an innocent kiss. At least, I thought it did. I was sad you'd left. He was comforting me."

"You could have pushed him away." Amber stopped the words that wanted to pour from her. She focused on releasing her anger. There was no way she wanted to let the panther escape.

"I was shocked. He kissed me. Properly. That was the last thing I expected. I know how much you love him."

"Not anymore."

"Loved him. I wouldn't hurt you. He's been telling

everyone we're dating. I've been denying it. He's been saying we don't want it to get back to you. Everyone believes him. I was terrified you would too."

Amber threw her arms around Crystal. "You idiot. Of course I wouldn't. I know you. I couldn't understand why you didn't tell me about this."

"I was confused. There are so many rumours flying about. The worst is that you're not coming back. Tell me that's not true."

"Crystal…" What could she say? She feared the same thing.

Crystal pulled away, standing to face her. "It's true, isn't it? Why didn't you tell me? Why'd you let me think it was only for a couple of months?"

Amber rose. "Because Mum lied to me. And I don't know for certain, but I think it might be true. Or it would be if I weren't going to uni next year. She can't keep me in Hicksville then."

Crystal giggled. "Hicksville?"

Amber smiled. "Yep."

Crystal threw her arms around Amber. "I've missed you so much. In future I promise to talk to you no matter how stupid I've been."

"You better."

"How'd you get here?"

"A friend gave me a lift." Amber forced herself not to hesitate over the last word.

"Friend?" Crystal's voice was uncertain.

"You have nothing to worry about. No one could take your place." Amber turned to scan the yard. Her gaze locked on Kade. When she saw he watched her, she beckoned him forward.

"Oh!" Crystal stared at Kade, speechless.

"Kade, this is Crystal."

"Is this who you've replaced Josh with?"

"How do you want me to play this, Amber?"

She was tempted, but her friendship with Crystal was worth more than that. "No. We're just… friends. Armed enemies sometimes, but mostly friends."

"A pity. That'd really burn Josh." Crystal grinned.

Amber couldn't resist grinning back. "Very tempting."

"I could go and get my phone to take a pic." Crystal glanced between them.

Kade shrugged. "It doesn't bother me."

"Wait right there." Crystal dashed back to her room.

"You don't have to." Amber turned to Kade.

"I know."

"Why are you?"

"I heard what you said. He's not worth tears. Focusing on revenge is a better choice."

"Why do I get the feeling that revenge is your answer to a lot of things?"

Kade grinned. "Survival of the fittest. That includes never showing weakness."

Crystal hurried towards them, phone held aloft. "I've got it. Get close."

Kade wrapped his arms around Amber, and pulled her against him so her back met his chest. He dipped his head so his mouth was close to her ear. "This is starting to become a habit."

Amber blinked at the bright flash. She turned her head slightly. "What is?"

"You using me to annoy other boys in your life."

"Justin isn't part of my life."

"He wanted to be." The flash went again.

"He wanted to win a bet."

"That was only a cover."

"How do you know for certain?"

Kade laughed softly. "Most humans are an open book. It's as simple as reading them." The flash went again. "Their scent. The way they hold themselves, speak, act. Body language can be as clear as words." Another flash.

"Great. Thanks. Those photos will be perfect. I

can't wait to rub his nose in them. I can tell everyone he lied about us so that when they found out about you two he wasn't left looking like the one dumped." Crystal tucked her phone in her bra. "How long can you stay?"

"A couple of minutes. I have to get home. I can't go sneaking in at daybreak, I might get caught." Amber reluctantly stepped out of Kade's arms. It had felt surprisingly right surrounded by them.

"I wish you didn't have to go."

"I don't want to. I didn't want to go in the first place."

"Will you come back and see me?"

Amber glanced at Kade who nodded slightly. "Yes. As soon as I can."

"I miss you. Nothing is the same without you about," Crystal said.

"I know. Nothing is the same for me either." Amber stepped forward to hug Crystal, trying not to think about how much things weren't the same. "Never do that to me again. I don't care what you've done. Tell me so we can get past it."

"I will. I promise."

When they were alone in front of Crystal's house, Kade looked around. "What now? Is that all you wanted to do?"

Amber smiled wryly. "I would like to say I need to go and punch Josh in the face, but that probably wouldn't be a good idea."

"I wouldn't mind taking you there. I hate disloyalty."

Amber was tempted. But she worried she might lose control and who knew what might happen. "I can't. What if I became a panther?"

"I'll keep an eye on you."

Amber thought about it for another minute. She shook her head. "No. It's best not to. Every time I think of him, I want to shred him with my claws. Even more so now I've spoken to Crystal."

"You aren't even curious about why he did it?"

"Yeah, but not enough to risk losing control. Can you take me back to my grandmother's house now?"

Kade nodded. "Let's find somewhere secluded."

Amber grinned. "That sounds like a pick up line."

"I don't need a pick up line. I'm coming home with you." His grin was pure trouble.

Amber opened her mouth to argue. She changed her mind. The last thing she felt like dealing with was a wyvern. Her freak abilities were unpredictable and since it was Kade's fault she had them, he should do guard duty. And she had school tomorrow. She needed some sleep to be able to cope with that.

"Are you going to continue to ignore me at school?"

Amber glanced towards Kade. "What?"

"Never mind. I guess I'll find out eventually."

Chapter Eleven

Late the next morning, Amber glared at Justin where he sat on the edge of her desk. She was beginning to wonder if he'd been to any of his own classes. Justin turned seventeen at the beginning of the year, his sister at the end. There was nearly twelve months between them. Although they were both in her year, she couldn't recall seeing them in any of her classes. Well, before today that was.

"I need to open my book." Amber kept up her glare.

"Then where will I sit?"

"How about in your own classroom?"

Justin grinned. "You've got such a great sense of humour."

Amber's hands gripped the edge of her desk as she tried to control herself. Her senses sharpened. Under the mix of smells that included soap, shampoo and deodorant, Amber could smell warm, sluggish prey.

"Amber!"

"I'm doing the best I can. Do you know how hard this is? I need something to eat and I've still got to get through this class before lunch. Why'd you have to land on my balcony that night?" She wished she had the ability to turn her fingernails into claws so she could dig them into Justin to get him moving.

"There's a party this Saturday night. Are you interested in going?" Justin rose to stand beside her desk. He leaned forward, one hand resting on the back of her chair.

"If you don't do something about this idiot, I swear I'll do something drastic, Kade."

"I'm nearly there. Hold on."

Amber opened her maths book. "Not interested." She glanced up as the classroom door opened. Hoping it was the teacher, she smiled when she saw it was Kade. Even better.

Justin turned to see who had entered. "What's he doing here?"

Amber slid from her chair and was in front of her desk by the time Kade reached her. He wrapped his arms around her and their lips met. The classroom receded. Her annoyance at Justin evaporated. She smiled up at Kade as he pulled back slightly.

"Is that what you were looking for?" Kade whispered.

Amber grinned. "Perfect."

"I'll see you at lunch. This might help until then." Kade pressed a chocolate bar into her hand before he lightly kissed her then strode from the classroom.

Amber opened the wrapper as she turned back to face Justin. He stared at her with an expression that could only be amazement. "As I've said a million times. I'm not interested." She took a bite of her chocolate.

"You didn't say you and Kade were seeing each other."

"It doesn't matter the reason. I'm not interested." She pushed past him to sit in her seat. The classroom door opened. This time it was the teacher.

Without another word, Justin left the room. Amber smiled as she leaned back in her seat and had another mouthful of chocolate. Her feet crossed at her ankles and her gaze met that of her teacher, Mr Carlton. He didn't look happy.

"Is this a classroom or a café?" Mr Carlton's hands went behind his back as he slowly walked towards her. The class fell silent.

Amber crammed the last piece of chocolate in her mouth and shrugged.

"I don't want to see you eating in my class again. Understand?"

Amber swallowed the chocolate and wished she had a drink to wash it down. "Sure." She bet he wouldn't still feel the same way if she turned into a panther and fed on his students.

Mr Carlton continued to stare at her a moment longer before he turned and walked towards the front of the classroom, hands still clasped behind his back. "Homework out. Hand it forward. Then go on with the pages written up on the board."

She wasn't the only one who groaned when they read the pages listed on the board.

* * *

Amber dropped her schoolbag just inside her bedroom. Kicking off her shoes, she locked the bedroom door and dropped onto her bed. The week had been far too long. She was glad it was Friday. Two blissful, school free days. Two days without idiots hanging out with her because she was with Kade. Two days without turning a corridor and finding yet another female with a hairstyle identical to hers, right down to the colour. What did they think? Becoming her clone would be the way to catch Kade's attention? Idiots!

She rose and restlessly paced. She had to get out of this town. Amber dropped onto the seat at her desk and turned on her laptop. Her head jerked up and she scented the air. A slight smile curved her lips.

"It's unlocked." She grinned as Kade entered the French doors. "Someone's going to notice you coming through my balcony doors one day."

Kade shrugged and dropped down on her bed, lying with his hands behind his head. "Do you think you can stay with us this weekend? All weekend? Your bed's far too small."

"There's always the floor," Amber said absently as she noticed Crystal was online.

"Ask."

"Hmm." She clicked on Crystal's name.

"Are you listening to me?"

"Not really."

Amber says: Hey.
Crystal says: Come home!!!!
Amber says: I wish.

Crystal says: Party tomorrow night. Wish you were going too.

Amber says: So do I. There's a lame one on here. Don't think I want to go.

Crystal says: Come here then. Stay the weekend. Pleeeeeeease.

Amber says: Got no way of getting there.

Crystal says: Catch a bus.

Kade leaned over her shoulder. "You can't stay there on your own. Only if Maira can sleep there too."

"Where would you be?" Amber looked up at him, their faces centimetres apart.

"About."

"Would you be in Brisbane too?" When Kade nodded in answer, Amber frowned. "Where would you stay?"

"We'd get a room somewhere."

"Why?"

"Because it isn't safe for you to be wandering around on your own."

"No, I meant why would you do that for me?" Amber ignored the beeps coming from her laptop.

"Would you normally go?"

"I'd try and convince my mum to let me go."

"Tell her Maira can drive you."

Amber smiled. "Thank you." She turned back to the laptop.

Crystal says: You still there?

Crystal says: Hello???

Crystal says: I didn't think it was that bad a suggestion.

Amber says: Sorry. Was talking to Kade. If Mum agrees to let me go can Maira sleep over too?

Crystal says: Shouldn't be a problem. Mum's fairly laid back about who I have over. Unless it's a boy. Why?

Amber says: She can give me a lift.

Crystal says: She there too?

Amber says: brb.

Amber turned to Kade again and tugged a lock of her hair from his fingers. "We don't have an audience."

Kade grinned. "I'm not that nice."

"Meaning?"

"Even to help you get the message through to Justin I wouldn't kiss you if I wasn't interested."

Amber stared at him, trying to think what she could say. Her gaze was drawn to his lips. The last thing she needed was more complications in her life. Her heart leapt. Obviously it didn't agree with her mind. She rose to her feet.

"Amber."

Gazes met. Held. Amber's lips parted, her mouth suddenly dry. Words failed. Her lips curved slightly. Words weren't always necessary. Reaching for him, her eyes closed as her lips met his and she was lost in a swirl of emotions. When a sound like a purr rose from her throat, she pulled back, eyes wide.

Sight, sound and smell were all heightened. Her skin felt tight and she knew how to bring forth the panther. It would take seconds. She forced it back down. It wasn't her. She was human.

"What's wrong?"

"I know how to change. I don't want to know that." Amber stepped back. "I'm human!"

"Change."

"What?"

"You need to know how to change. What if you accidentally change into a panther? You need to know how to change back at will. You also need to recognise the signs of when you're going to change and how to stop it."

Amber stared at him. "Change. Into a panther."

"Unless you can manage a dragon, panther will do." Kade smiled fleetingly.

"Fine!" She pulled off her uniform, standing in leather shorts and a bikini top. She turned her back on Kade. His gaze was too distracting. She called forth the panther, feeling her skin tighten and senses heighten. She stretched out her arms and stared at her hands. She smiled as she recalled wanting to turn her fingernails into claws. She watched them change. She tried to hold it there. It was impossible. The changes continued, like a tremor through her body.

"Now talk to me." Kade reached out and ran his hand along the fur on her back.

Amber growled in annoyance.

Kade shook his head. *"Talk to me."*

Seconds passed until they turned into minutes. Amber finally figured out how to control the animal mind that wanted to swamp the human one. *"Happy?"*

"Try a sentence."

"Just don't expect me to recite Shakespeare."

Kade laughed. "Okay. Change back now."

It took nearly a minute before Amber could reverse the process. She stretched as she rose to stand on two feet. Her hands ran down her arms, surprisingly smooth after being covered by fur, fighting back an urge to do a victory dance. She didn't want the ability to turn into a panther. It wasn't like she could tell anyone. Turning into a dragon would have been more practical. Then she could've flown anywhere she wanted to go. She could have visited Crystal.

"How do you feel?" Kade took her hand in his.

"Only half human."

Kade tugged her closer. "Join the club. Now, how about you get dressed and see what your mother has to say about going to the city for the weekend?"

Amber nodded, pulling her hand away. "Don't hold your breath though. She's not real happy with me."

"What'd you do?"

"I got annoyed with my grandmother. Stupid old woman. She was hassling me. If they thought I was going to sit there and take it, they were kidding themselves." She pulled a dress on over her head. "I'm not sure how long it'll take me."

"I'm not going anywhere."

It took Amber nearly half an hour. She returned to her room with a grin. Locking the door behind her, she lost her grin when she saw Kade was at her laptop typing. He looked up as she stalked across the room.

"Don't worry, I told Crystal it was me. I was bored sitting here waiting for you. So was she."

Amber scrolled up to skim through what he'd written. Nothing important. Mainly what classes he was in and where he lived. Basic information she already had. "I need my seat back."

"I take it you can go?"

Amber nodded as she took Kade's place in front of the laptop.

Amber says: I'm back. Can I stay for the weekend?

Crystal says: When do you get here?

Amber says: Tomorrow. Tried for tonight, but she expects me to get homework out of the way first : (

Crystal says: Good thing you're not here right now. Your ears would be bleeding from my scream of excitement!!!

Amber says: I'll be there as soon as possible. Your parents okay with two extra bodies Saturday night?

Crystal says: Yep. Already checked with them. They wanted to know if Maira's parents want to talk to them. Said to give them our number.

Amber says: That's not an issue. They don't live with their parents.

Crystal says: You never said that!!

Amber says: Sorry.

Crystal says: You're not going to have time to sleep tomorrow night. I have a million questions to ask.

Amber says: Me too. I want to know everything that's happened since I've been gone.

Crystal says: No problem.

Amber says: g2g. Need to get my homework done or I can't come.

Crystal says: K. See you tomorrow. I can't wait.

Amber says: Me too

Crystal says: Bibi.

Amber says: Later.

Amber turned to Kade. "Are you sure Maira will be able to go?"

Kade grinned. "Don't tell me you've already forgotten she has to follow orders?"

"You mean you can tell her how to spend her free time? Even what parties to attend?"

"They don't get free time. I guess you could say they're always on call."

"That's barbaric."

"I never claimed it wasn't."

Amber could only shake her head. "Don't expect blind obedience from me."

Kade laughed softly. "I wouldn't dream of it."

Chapter Twelve

The music vibrated around them. Amber couldn't stop grinning. She was in her own city, amongst friends. She'd missed this. She glanced around. There wasn't much space to dance in the press of bodies. Many couples were plastered against each other, like Maira and Brann were. Amber was dancing in a group that included Crystal, Kade and Angela.

A new scent entered the room and Amber met Kade's gaze. His body was no longer relaxed. If she hadn't spent so much time with him, she wouldn't have noticed. *"Dragon, isn't it?"*

Kade nodded, stepping closer to her. *"We have to get out of here."*

"Why?"

Brann and Maira appeared at their side. "I'm starving. Let's go get something to eat." Maira smiled easily at the crowd. "And not the chips and stuff sitting in the other room. I want real food."

Kade nodded. "Are you coming, Amber?"

She could see the order in Kade's eyes. "Sure. I could eat a horse… or deer."

"Aww, stay. You were going to spend every second of this weekend with me," Crystal protested.

"She can't come." Kade continued to stare at Amber. *"Deal with this. Quickly."*

"We'll be back," Amber said.

"Then I'm coming too." Crystal linked her arm through Amber's.

"Me too." Angela took Amber's other arm.

"There's not room for six in the car." Kade kept glancing behind Amber.

Amber wanted to check what he was looking at. She managed to stay focused on Crystal and Angela instead. "We won't be long. You know I don't take forever to eat."

"There's room for me," Crystal said stubbornly.

Amber managed to bite back a sigh. She looked at Kade. *"She won't budge. We'll have to take her with us. We'll be standing here arguing for ages if we don't."* He nodded slightly and turned away, pushing through the bodies in the room. "I'll catch you later, Inge."

Amber hugged her friend before she turned back to Crystal. "Come on then. Let's go eat."

They were nearly out of the house when they ran into Josh and a handful of his mates. Anger surged through Amber. She felt her skin tighten and forced herself to relax. She couldn't change into a panther in a room full of people. Especially since she knew most of them. *"Kade!"* She sent a picture of Josh blocking her way.

"Look who's returned to Brisbane. Weren't you moving permanently?"

"Get out of my way, Josh." Amber glared at him.

"Is that any way to talk to your boyfriend?"

"You've been replaced."

"I don't see him anywhere."

"Then how about you turn around and look." Kade came through the crowd to stand behind Josh, who spun to face him.

Josh took a step back and to the side so he could see both of them. "You said you'd be gone two months. Your mother was telling her friends she wasn't coming back this year. I don't appreciate being lied to."

Amber moved to stand beside Kade, Crystal's arm still linked in hers. Kade draped his arm around her shoulders. "I never lied to you. I told you all the information I was given. But it doesn't matter now. You should have talked to me first." She started to move away.

"Amber." Josh reached out for her.

Amber pushed his hand away. "Leave me alone. Are you blind? Can't you see you've been replaced?"

"I wouldn't have–" Josh began.

"You're a complete bastard, Josh. And neither of us wants anything to do with you," Crystal interrupted him.

"Amber–"

"You heard Crystal. Now back off." Amber took another few steps and was outside, Crystal and Kade still one on either side of her.

Josh followed, leaving his friends behind. "Or what? Your boyfriend will knock me out?"

"I don't need anyone to fight my battles for me. You want someone to knock you out? Then come closer and let me have a go." Amber shrugged Kade and Crystal off, stepping away from them.

Josh laughed. He stepped close and tapped the side of his chin. "Give it your best shot. You can't even hit a ball with a cricket bat. Your threat's empty."

Amber felt her skin tighten. Adrenaline rushed through her. She could smell the other dragon coming closer. They had minutes to get out of here.

Strength filled her limbs and she barely held the panther back. She wanted to pounce on him, rip him to shreds. Carve up the smirk on his face. Instead, she swung at him. She could feel the panther trying to crawl out, take over. Her fist connected with Josh's chin, he landed on the ground and his mouth dropped open.

Kade's arms wrapped around her and his mouth was near her ear. "Back down. You're human Amber, and we've got to get out of here. Now."

Amber struggled against the panther. Sweat broke out on her forehead. "Stay out of my way, Josh." She turned away from him, walking beside Kade. She glanced at Crystal on her other side. Her friend looked dazed. Reaching out a hand, she squeezed Crystal's, focusing on the humanness of her. The panther retreated. Amber relaxed slightly.

Maira had the car double parked in the street, the engine running. Brann was in the front with her. The three of them piled into the back, with Amber in the middle. She buckled up, pretending not to see the looks Crystal kept sending her way.

Maira let off the handbrake and put the car into gear. "Any suggestions before I die of starvation?"

Amber gave directions to the closest café, which also served meals, and then closed her eyes. They popped open and she looked upwards. She opened her mouth, forgetting this wasn't something she could share with Crystal. Kade's hand tightened on hers and she looked towards him. He shook his head slightly. Amber looked up again and then back at him.

Kade smiled at her. *"I know. But there's not much we can do while your friend is with us. Relax for now. He's only tracking us. He's probably curious."*

"Has he tried to contact you?"

"Only tried to barge in. Keep your shields up. It's the only reason I know he's still up there. He keeps trying to find a way into my mind."

Kade had spent the past week teaching her how to block people from reading her mind. She wasn't perfect at it, but could hold out long enough until Kade could help shore up her defences. *"Okay."* She started to ask Kade why she could sense the dragon above them even though he wasn't trying to invade her mind, but Crystal spoke.

"What happened back there?"

Amber grinned. "Josh landed on his butt."

Crystal laughed. "I know that part. And as much as I loved every second of it, you can't hit a ball that's thrown directly at a bat you're holding. You hit him on the exact spot he tapped. What have you been doing?"

"Self-defence classes with me," Maira said.

"Really?" Crystal glanced between Maira and Amber.

"It's boring going to things like that on my own. And it's not like these two would be comfortable going to a women's self defence class." Maira grinned, meeting Crystal's gaze in the rear view mirror.

"I wouldn't have thought you'd learn something like that." Crystal looked at Amber carefully. "And why didn't you tell me?"

Amber could only shrug. *"Thanks, Maira. We know each other too well to be able to lie without the other picking up on it."*

"Promise me you'll tell me everything in future?" Crystal rested her hand on Amber's arm. "Please? I don't want us to grow apart. I hate that your mum dragged you away."

"I hope you're not expecting her to tell you absolutely everything." Kade ran his finger down Amber's cheek. "I'd have to protest that promise." He smiled. "I'd end up with performance anxiety."

Maira laughed. "Yeah sure. Your ego wouldn't allow it."

"Ego! You act like that's a bad thing," Kade said.

"Nah, it couldn't be." Brann shook his head, a slight grin as he turned towards the backseat.

Maira rolled her eyes. "Men! I'm constantly surrounded by testosterone."

Brann reached out to rest his hand on her thigh. "But you love it."

"Not when there's five of you at home."

"Five!" Crystal exclaimed. She turned to Amber. "Didn't you say you stayed at Maira's place?"

Amber nodded, relieved the conversation topic had changed. "Yeah, but don't mention to anyone that five guys live there too. Mum'd freak if she found out."

"I can't believe you pulled that one off. Sleeping over at a house with five guys in it!"

Amber grinned. "And no parents."

"So unfair," Crystal muttered.

Amber laughed. "Well, if you ever met Flinn, you probably wouldn't be so excited by the idea. He's worse than Josh. Someone needs to knock him to the ground."

Maira burst into laughter.

"Who?" Amber demanded. When Maira stopped laughing abruptly, she could only think it was because Kade had ordered her to shut up. She turned to him. "Why?"

"Because he annoys me."

Amber's eyes narrowed. "Try again."

"Shut up, Amber. Your friend's listening to every word."

"Tell me!"

"You aren't part of our society. He shouldn't have left you to face the wyvern." Kade smiled wryly. "Drop it. If you can."

"Midnight snack time." Maira parked the car. "Big, fat, juicy steak."

Amber's mouth watered. "Stop tormenting me."

As they stepped into the café, Crystal lightly touched Amber on the arm to get her attention. "You've changed."

Amber stopped, just inside the door. Kade hovered near her while Maira and Brann went to order food. "I'm still me."

Crystal shook her head. "I'm not sure how, but you're different. It's... I don't know... like someone else has invaded your body."

"Don't be silly."

"I don't know how else to describe it. When you hit Josh, it was like you were someone else. And a few minutes ago when you were thinking of eating. What's going on?"

Amber sighed. "I'm still me."

"I thought we were best friends. That we shared everything."

Kade took a step closer. Amber shook her head as she met his gaze. "Give us a minute." She took Crystal's hand, dragging her over to a table in the corner. They sat across from each other.

"Don't you dare tell her," Kade warned.

"Back off. I'm not stupid. Order me a steak. Medium. And a salad for Crystal."

"Are you going to tell me what's going on?" Crystal asked.

Amber shook her head. "I'm sorry, but I can't. I've stumbled onto someone else's secret and I've promised to keep it. I wish I could tell you. You know I would if it was possible."

"Kade's secret? Is that why you said something about being enemies sometimes? Is he... I don't know... threatening you? Blackmailing you?"

"No! It isn't like that. I didn't want to know his secret and it was his fault I found out. An accident, but his fault all the same."

"Should I be worried about you?"

Amber's laugh was brittle. "I really don't know. I'm not meant to know his secret. I guess you could call it a life and death one."

"Amber-"

"Now can you understand why, even though I can't, I also don't want to share it with you? I don't want to put you at risk too."

"What can I do to help?"

"Nothing. Just stay my friend. Even if I can't tell you everything anymore."

"Always."

"And don't treat Kade like a leper. He's doing the best he can."

Crystal smiled. "You know me too well." Her smile faded. "I thought you said the two of you were only friends. But, you really like him, don't you?"

Amber glanced over at the table Kade, Maira and Brann sat at. He was watching her. Her lips slowly curved into a smile, which he answered with one of his own. She turned back to Crystal.

"You don't need to answer. I can see you do."

Even though she knew Kade could probably hear her, Crystal deserved some kind of answer. Particularly since there was so much else she couldn't share with her. "Sometimes I feel like punching him like I did Josh. Other times I feel like dragging him off to the closest bedroom. He annoys the hell out of me, makes me laugh, drives me insane, makes me feel like I could fly to the moon and I miss him when he's not with me."

"You love him."

Amber shrugged. "I thought I loved Josh. Look how that turned out."

"He's different from Josh. Dangerous. But I don't think he'd ever hurt you. You know that movie we watched, the one with the sword fighting and I said a man like that would die for his woman?" Crystal waited for Amber to nod. "That's who he makes me think of. A warrior."

"That's how I think of him too."

Crystal glanced at the other table. "Do you think I could stay with you next weekend? I could catch a bus Friday afternoon. I looked into it."

"I don't know. I want you to, but I don't want to risk you getting involved. I thought it'd be safe for me to see you here, but now I'm not so sure. I've got a bad feeling we brought some of the problems with us."

"I don't care. Friends face problems together."

"Crystal-"

"Together."

Amber sighed. "I'll think about it. I'm not putting you in danger because I miss spending time with you."

"How dangerous can Hicksville be?"

Amber smiled slightly when Crystal used her name for the town. "You'd be surprised." She glanced over to Kade again. "Come on, let's go and eat. The food's arrived."

"I didn't order anything." Crystal rose to her feet.

"There's a salad over there with your name on it."

Crystal linked her arm through Amber's. "See. We know each other perfectly. We need to stick together. Who else is going to look out for you like I would?"

They reached the table and Amber sat in front of the large steak that was the same as those in front of the other three. Crystal stared at the food, looking from hers to Amber's.

Amber met Crystal's gaze. "Maybe not perfectly anymore. I'm sorry."

Crystal looked at the steak that would normally have a salad on the side and only take up half the space it did. "So am I."

Chapter Thirteen

Sitting in the backseat of Maira's car, Amber leaned against Kade, wishing the weekend didn't have to end. Or that she had to return to her grandmother's house. But she had school tomorrow.

"Pull over at the rest area ahead," Kade ordered Maira. "And stay with Amber. Take her home."

Amber noticed the dragon from Saturday night was still flying above them. He had followed them the entire drive from the city and he wasn't alone. There were three of them up there. "I'm not going to leave you behind."

"I'll have Brann with me."

"Two against three. Not good odds."

"Amber–"

"No! I won't have you risk yourself so Maira can get me to safety."

"I don't know who's up there. I can't have them

finding out about you. They aren't young dragons. Or at least one of them isn't. I had a sense of quite a few years when he tried to invade my mind. At least fifty years. Maybe even a hundred."

"I'll stay in the car. You take Maira with you. I'll be fine."

Kade stared at her thoughtfully. "Don't go looking for trouble."

Amber smiled. "I never go looking for trouble. It has a tendency to come after me."

Kade frowned. "That's why-"

"Kade! I'll be fine. I'll lock the doors and wait for you."

Maira pulled up at the rest area, parking as far from the road as possible. "So, what's the plan? All?"

Kade hesitated. Then he nodded. "All." He unbuttoned his shirt and dropped it on the seat. "Lock the car and don't go anywhere." He pulled Amber to him, kissing her before he got out of the car.

Amber watched as the three of them shimmered into dragons and took to the sky. She loved watching them do that. Locking the car, she slid into the front passenger's seat. For some reason it felt safer in there. It was probably because she had a better view of her surroundings. Winding the window down slightly, she breathed deep, picking up the scents in the area.

Three familiar dragons, three strange ones. Reaching out with her mind, she felt them out there. They moved further away. She didn't try to invade any of their minds. She wasn't good enough for that. All she wanted to do was keep track of where they were.

The window of the driver's door shattered, a fist reached for the keys, dragging Amber's attention back. She stared at the hand in shock for a few seconds before fear kicked in and had her moving. Unlocking the passenger door, she jumped out. Pulling her shirt over her head, she threw it into the car through the still open door. If she had to change into a panther to escape, she didn't want to have to explain to her mother yet another missing garment.

A man moved towards Amber, the car keys dangling in his hands. He grinned at her and threw them into the bushes at the side of the road. "What are you?"

Amber slowly retreated, warily watching him. She hadn't even noticed him coming. She'd been too focused on the six dragons in the sky. For a split second she considered calling Kade, but she didn't know what was happening up there. She wasn't going to risk distracting him.

"Don't you mean who?"

The man laughed. "I don't care who you are. It's

the 'what' I want to know. We thought you were a young dragon at first. But there's a mixture of smells. Prey, predator. Human, dragon. Something I can't quite put my finger on. So what are you?"

Amber tried to ignore how much taller he was than her. How the muscles in his arms rippled when they moved and how broad his chest was. His legs were encased in dragon-leather. He looked to be in his thirties, but gave an impression of being much older. It was his eyes. Pale blue eyes that looked like they'd seen and experienced everything.

Fear skittered through Amber and she tried to rein in the panther. She'd learned it wasn't only hunger that made her want to change. Strong emotions of any kind did. "I don't know what you're going on about."

"Cat. I can smell cat."

"Probably ferals in the area."

"Come here, little kitty."

Amber felt a tree at her back. She stepped to the side so she could retreat further. "Get away from me."

"What's wrong, kitty?"

Amber was glad cats could see in the dark as she stepped further into the trees at the edge of the rest area. She almost laughed when the thought of being late home and risking being grounded popped into her mind. That was the least of her problems. She didn't even know if she'd make it home.

"Come on, kitty. Come quietly and I'll call my people back and leave yours alone. Make things difficult…" he let the threat hang in the air.

Amber took a deep breath. Surely they could take care of themselves. Maybe. She ran up against barbed wire and quickly slipped through the strands of the fence and into an open paddock.

The man followed. "My patience is wearing thin. Now, what are you?"

"Human."

"You lie." The man leapt towards her, transforming into a dragon. Claws aimed at her, a blue and silver dragon attached to them.

Amber raised her hands. Balls of fire struck the dragon. He faltered and Amber leapt to the side, fire sitting in her palms, ready to be thrown again. She reminded herself to thank Kade for making her practice how to call the fire to her hands.

The dragon roared, landing on the ground as a human. "Where's your Gold Warrior? Is he one of the ones up there?" He pointed skyward.

Amber shook her head.

"Why are Dragon Mages being made again? Who's making them? How are they making them?"

Amber continued to retreat. The man continued to stalk forward. "None of your business."

"I'm making it my business. Now start talking, mage."

Amber wanted answers. This man had them. She couldn't see him willingly giving them to her. "What's your name?"

"Ronan. What's yours?"

She hesitated then guessed it was only fair. "Amber."

"Where's your Gold Warrior, Amber?"

"Why do you keep asking that?"

"I'm not stupid. A Dragon Mage can't exist without a Gold Warrior."

Amber ignored the fear that comment brought. Can't exist? Because it took a Gold Warrior to make one or because they died when the dragon did? She pushed that thought from her mind. She had far too many other problems to deal with right now. "What's it to you, anyway?"

"Because I want my own Dragon Mage. You come with me and I'll leave your friends alone. Help me take my lands back and afterwards you can return to your own dragon. Which powers do you have?"

Why did Ronan know about Dragon Mages when Kade didn't? "How old are you?"

He shrugged. "Five, six centuries. Maybe more. Who pays attention to time when that much passes?"

Amber barely managed to control her shock. Dragons could live that long? All dragons? She didn't have enough information to deal with Ronan. She was floundering. "Why would I want to help you?"

Ronan sniffed the air. "It was strange of you to choose a cat for your animal. Most mages are more practical. Hawk, owl, falcon. Something they can turn into if they should lose their seat. Why a cat?"

Choose. Amber was intrigued. Was it because of the cat hairs? Could she have picked something else instead? How? Would she be able to change what animal she could turn into? There were so many questions she wanted answered. But she didn't trust Ronan. "Quit trying to come close to me. Do you think I'm going to want to listen to anything you have to say when you're doing that?"

Ronan stood still. "I'll give you my heir. He has no mate. When I have my lands back, they'll be his one day."

Mail order groom? Not in this lifetime. But she couldn't tell Ronan that. "I'm not patient enough to wait for your death."

Ronan laughed. "A couple of centuries and I'll be too old for battles. I'll retire then."

"I don't like to share. Not interested."

"I'll help you take your own lands. Gold. Jewels. Name your price."

She frantically tried to think of a way to escape. Nothing came to mind other than to keep him talking. "How did you lose your lands?"

"Treachery." He shrugged. "It wasn't the first time. But this time I haven't been able to take them back. Which clan do you belong to?"

Clan! Amber bit back the hysterical laugh that wanted to escape. She felt like she was trying to find her way through an oil slick. She didn't know how much longer she could stay on her feet. "I have all I need. I'm not interested in any of your offers." Didn't trust them, was more accurate.

"Are you saying there isn't a single thing in all the worlds that you want?"

Worlds! She had to keep him talking. She was learning more by the second. Intriguing scraps of information. She wasn't certain how they fit together, but it would give her more things to ask Kade about. "I have simple wants."

"That I don't believe. I can see from here the quality of leather used for your clothes. They wouldn't have been cheap. Unless you're from one of the clans who make them."

"They were a gift from a friend."

"You're not the only one with powerful friends. I will have you. Join me willingly and life will be much better for you."

"Amber! Where are you? What happened to waiting in the car?"

Amber felt a wave of relief at Kade's angry words. She sent a picture of where she was, Ronan standing in front of her.

Kade swore. *"Get away from him. He's a renegade."*

"What caused you to become a renegade?" Amber asked.

"I don't see myself as one. Besides, I'll be accepted once I have my lands again." Ronan shrugged. "We're a practical race."

"That doesn't answer my question."

"Amber! Get away from him now."

"Because cannibalism has been outlawed. They say we live long enough without needing to eat the hearts of our enemies. I was eating them long before they brought in their stupid law. I couldn't stop without losing all the benefits I'd gained. A couple of centuries are nothing compared to how long it's possible to live by eating them. What would you have done?"

Certainly not eat someone's heart, but she wasn't

about to tell Ronan that. "Who knows? I haven't been faced with that choice."

"I'll bring you the heart of the next dragon I slay. Then we'll see what choice you make."

Kade landed beside Amber. Brann and Maira dropped down behind him. They became human the moment they touched the ground. "Stay away from her."

"You're Kiani's boy. I see her look in you. Who's your sire?"

"Bredon."

"Erilan Clan?"

When Kade nodded, Ronan looked at Amber. "You keep high company. Is he your Gold Warrior or is it one of his parents?"

"What's going on?" Kade didn't take his gaze off Ronan. *"And get rid of that fire in your hands."*

Amber closed her hands, extinguishing the fire. "It doesn't matter who my dragon is, I'm not interested in your offer. You'll have to find someone else to help you get your lands back. I have other things keeping me busy."

"Who are Erilan Clan going to war with? How many Dragon Mages do they have? When will it happen?" Ronan looked from Amber to Kade.

"That isn't any of your business. Leave us alone.

Go and help your people. They aren't doing too well. My clan knows you've met with us. I wouldn't do anything or you'll have the entire clan after you. Think they'll be willing to give up their mage?" Kade smiled mockingly.

Ronan stared at him a moment longer. "This isn't over. I'd watch your backs if I were you." He became a dragon and shot into the sky.

Kade turned to Amber. "What the hell were you thinking? Are you mad? He's even eaten the heart of one of his sons. Do you think someone like that is sane?"

"You wear the skin of dragons. What's the difference?"

"Would you eat a dragon heart if he brought it to you?"

Amber shook her head, taking a step back from Kade. She'd never seen him so angry. Or look so dangerous. "I didn't know how to answer him. I'm not crazy. I was trying to stay alive."

"You were grilling him for information."

"Maybe." It wasn't like he told her anything.

"Get back in the car."

"He threw the keys."

"Go and find them."

Amber glared at Kade. "You find them." She spun,

striding across the paddock. There was a slight tremor in her limbs as fear gave way to relief. Her eyes watered and she blinked. "Damn night air," she muttered.

"Amber–"

"Leave me alone, Kade."

Kade grabbed her arm, pulling her roughly against him. He pressed her head to his chest. "I was terrified I wouldn't get to you in time."

Chapter Fourteen

Amber's nose was filled with the smell of blood. She pulled away from Kade, her gaze scanning his body. "You're hurt?"

"A scratch."

"Where?"

"Amber-"

"Where?"

Kade turned. "A scratch."

Amber gasped at the gash that went from one shoulder to the opposite hip. Blood seeped from it. "You have to-"

Kade faced her again. "Forget it. If I let Maira stitch me I won't be able to transform again tonight. Not with that many stitches. Come on. We have to get out of here before Ronan comes back."

"At least let someone clean it up."

"Fine. There's a first aid kit in the car."

They strode to the car in silence. Maira had the kit sitting on the bonnet when they arrived back, Brann's leather backpack open beside it. She quickly wiped the blood away and frowned as she inspected the wounds.

"What are you doing?" Amber asked when Maira removed the belt from her pants.

"Hold the edges of this deepest section together. The belt should stop it from gaping too much when he transforms."

Amber pressed her hands against Kade's skin and then moved them together so the jagged edges of his wound met. It looked worse now the blood had been wiped away. A trickle of blood seeped from the lower part of the wound. Amber pressed her hand against the spot, trying to hold it together as best she could so it'd stop bleeding. It felt like a shock from static electricity.

Kade swore, pulling away from her. "What do you think you're doing?"

Maira inspected Kade's back. "Whatever it was, do it again."

"Not likely!" Kade rounded on Maira.

"It's sealed," Amber gasped.

"What?" Kade reached behind him, gingerly

touching where Amber had placed her hand against his wound. He met Amber's gaze. "Do it again."

"I don't know what I did. I was worried about the blood still coming from your wound. I placed my hand on it and tried to stop it from bleeding."

"Found the keys." Brann strode towards them holding the keys up. He looked at each of them. "What's going on?"

"Our mage is healing Kade." Maira took the keys from Brann.

"No I'm not. And don't call me that. I'm not a mage."

"Ronan is one of our oldest people. If he says you're a Dragon Mage, then that's more than likely what you are. Now heal my back so I can get up there and we can put some distance between us and Ronan." Kade gestured towards the star studded sky.

Amber sighed heavily. "Sometimes I really hate you," she muttered as she placed her hand on his back.

"No you don't. Now stop sulking and figure out what you did last time. We're out of here in five minutes, wound or not."

Amber emptied her mind, mimicking her actions from before. Nothing. She concentrated on the blood. The smell of it filled her senses and her mouth watered. She frowned in disgust as she pushed the panther away. Electricity. That's what it had felt like. As if she'd welded it together. Energy instead of heat in her hands. She yelped as the energy flowed between them.

Kade turned, throwing his arms around her. He grinned. "I knew you could do it." He kissed her quickly. "You can finish it later. That was the worst of it." He pulled away, leaping into the sky and becoming a dragon before Amber even had a chance to think let alone speak.

Maira straightened from brushing the glass off the driver's seat. "Everyone in. Let's see how fast this car can move. Kade says it's all clear ahead."

"All clear?" Amber sat in the back of the car. She stared at the blood on her hands.

Brann threw her a damp cloth from where he sat in the front passenger seat. "No police, speed cameras or other drivers in the way."

Maira grinned. "Better buckle up."

Amber wiped her hands and quickly pulled the seat belt on. She glanced at the speedo and looked away as the needle kept moving even though it had reached a hundred kilometres. Did she really want to know how fast they were going? Wind rushed in at her from the broken window. Scents bombarded her. But she couldn't smell any strange dragons. Only

Kade was out there. She hoped it stayed that way. She looked down at her hands. Her hands that could kill and heal. What other surprises would they have for her? She closed her eyes, and her mind. No more thinking. Life was far too complicated. She felt like throwing something and screaming. She didn't want this. None of it. Got a life, like it, going back. Yeah, right! She was beginning to think that was an impossibility.

An image of Ronan standing in front of her staring at her with his pale blue eyes came to mind. He'd called her a Dragon Mage. She had no idea what that meant, but had a bad feeling it would only bring more problems.

* * *

The school bell rang. Students hurriedly gathered their books and rushed towards the door. Amber continued to sit. Even her teacher left without a backwards glance. Last class Friday. Who'd be crazy enough to sit in an empty classroom when the weekend was calling?

Amber dropped her head onto the book that was still open on her desk. Obviously she was. Three weeks she'd been stuck in Hicksville. Three long weeks. And the past week had been the worst. She couldn't sleep, couldn't focus in class and dreaded the training sessions Kade forced her to endure. He was determined to find out the exact extent of her abilities. He'd picked apart every word Ronan had spoken to her. He even had a friend researching Dragon Mages in the library of his clan. Actually, he called the person a cousin. But it didn't mean the same as it would when she called someone cousin. It meant they were part of his clan. And that was why Maira called him cousin. She was from his clan. Brann was from another clan. Kade had chosen Brann at Maira's request. They'd been together for over a year before Maira had joined Kade.

The scrape of a chair on the floor brought Amber's head up. She watched as Kade sat at the desk next to her, his chair turned to face her. "I can't do this anymore. I'm exhausted."

"Come camping with us?"

Amber frowned. "What?"

"Tents, sleeping bags, campfire. What do you say?"

"No lessons?"

"No lessons." Kade grinned. "Camping and hunting."

"I'm not eating raw meat."

Kade shrugged. "You can cook your kill if you want."

"You expect me to catch my own food?"

Kade laughed. "No need to look so outraged." He leaned close. "Let your panther out and see what she wants to do. A wild animal shouldn't be caged all the time. They'll try and break free if they are."

Amber felt her skin tighten. Heat and energy rushed through her hands. The thought of hunting for her own meals was far more tempting than she liked. "I'll ask my mum and see what she says. Don't hold your breath though."

"You'll figure it out if you really want to go." Kade rose to his feet, holding out his hand.

Amber took it, letting him pull her to her feet. She looked up at him, a shiver going through her at the expression on his face. His gaze was hotter than the fire she could hold in her hands. Amber draped her arms around his neck and smiled up at him in anticipation. She didn't have long to wait.

Minutes passed before Kade pulled back to gaze down at her. His voice was husky. "Gather up your gear and I'll give you a lift home. We'll leave this arve if you can."

"Okay. How are we getting there?"

Kade grinned. "Flying."

"I'm not sitting in that harness for hours on end."

"You won't have to. I've got a surprise for you."

Amber grabbed her books. "What?"

"You'll have to wait and see."

They walked towards the door. "That's so unfair. You know I hate surprises."

"No you don't. You just hate having to wait for them."

Chapter Fifteen

Amber slammed her bedroom door behind her. She locked it and looked towards her bed where she'd planned to sulk. Kade was lying in the middle, hands behind his head, waiting for her.

"When did you get in here?"

"About the time you screamed at your mother that she was unrealistic, wanted to lock you away in a nunnery and didn't trust you."

"Move over." She dropped onto the bed next to him. "I told you she probably wouldn't let me go."

Kade leaned up on an elbow to stare down at her. "Are you going to let that stop you?"

"What are you saying?" Amber looked at him suspiciously. "Are you asking me to run away for the weekend?"

"What's the worst she's going to do?"

"Ground me for life." Amber laughed. "As if that's

going to be much of a loss in this town." She sat up. "Besides, I'll be seventeen in a month and a half. Nearly an adult. I'm sick of her treating me like a kid."

"Are you walking out the front door or sneaking out the balcony?"

Amber grabbed a small cloth backpack, threw a change of leather clothes in it, grabbed her toiletries, brush and a towel. "I'm not sure." She paused and frowned. "I haven't got a sleeping bag."

"You can share mine."

"Think again."

Kade laughed. "We have a spare one you can use. Maira said they'd be out the front in about fifteen minutes. Is that fine or do you want her to park down the road?"

Finished packing, Amber stared at Kade thoughtfully. She smiled slightly and moved away to turn her laptop on.

"What are you thinking of?"

Amber shook her head. She quickly typed a message for Crystal, Angela and Jasper then emailed it. When Kade laughed, she looked up at him. "Will you stop reading my emails over my shoulder all the time?" She turned off the laptop and took it to the bathroom.

"Now what are you doing?"

"Hiding my laptop so she can't take it off me." She pointed to the manhole in the ceiling. "Do you think you can help me get it up there?"

"Hop on my shoulders." Kade bent down.

Seated on Kade's shoulders, Amber pushed the manhole cover aside and slid her laptop and power cord in to rest on the beams. She manoeuvred the cover back into place. As soon as she was on her feet again, Amber closed her eyes. She pictured her mother and grandmother in her mind and tried to figure out where they were. She thought her mother was in her bedroom, her grandmother in the kitchen. Not good. Not completely bad either.

"What are you doing?"

Amber opened her eyes. "I think my mum's in her bedroom and Grandma is in the kitchen."

"You can sense that?"

"Maybe. It might be wishful thinking. Well, not the part about Grandma in the kitchen."

Kade grinned. "Maira's pulling up out the front. Why don't we go down and see?"

"You can go out the balcony. I'm not having them check on me in my room all the time. I'll meet you out the front." She handed her backpack to him and grabbed her handbag. "Come rescue me if I take too long?"

"Definitely." He kissed her quickly then strode towards the French doors, disappearing behind the curtains.

Amber checked where her family were. Still in the same places. Maybe. She quietly opened her door and moved silently down the stairs. She wished there was another way out other than through the kitchen. Having both the front and back doors in the lounge room wasn't the best idea. What if there was ever a fire in there? How were they meant to get out?

"Where do you think you're going?" Helen demanded when Amber stepped into the kitchen.

"Camping."

"Your mother told you no."

"And I told her I was going." Amber crossed the kitchen and paused in the lounge room doorway. "I'll see you Sunday night."

"Don't you dare step out of this house!"

"See you, Grandma." Behind her, Amber could hear Helen bellowing for her daughter. She smiled as she stepped outside and saw Kade holding the back door of the car open for her. Hurrying forward, she hopped in, looking out the back window as Maira pulled away from the curb. She watched as her mother ran to the edge of the footpath. Amber faced forward. The expression on her mother's face did not indicate a good night Sunday. Taking her mobile phone from her handbag, she turned it off, ignoring Kade's laughter.

When they pulled up in front of Kade's home, Flinn came out to lean against a post of the verandah. He watched as they piled out of the car, glancing at the gear dumped on the floorboards near the front door.

"What are you planning?" Flinn gestured towards the gear.

"That hasn't anything to do with you. I thought you were going away this weekend." Kade stayed near the car, putting his arm around Amber.

Flinn's eyes narrowed. "I think it's time you found somewhere else to live. I don't want to be dragged into anything if the wyverns get her."

Kade shrugged. "You're welcome to move out any time. And you might as well. There won't be a Pliethin in this area for months."

"You'd like that, wouldn't you? I will manage a year in one place without drawing undue attention to myself." Flinn pushed away from the verandah post and strode towards them.

"Stay here," Kade muttered with a glance at

Amber. He moved forward to meet Flinn. "You'll have the place to yourself this weekend."

"What did the Pliethin do to you? And what did it do to her? Don't tell me nothing otherwise there's no reason for her to be wearing dragon-leather clothes." Flinn stared at Amber over Kade's shoulder.

"Stay out of my mind, Flinn. You won't catch me unaware," Kade said.

"Then answer me. What did the Pliethin do to her? She smells different."

"Will you two knock it off? I don't want to be setting up camp in the dark." Maira stepped between them. "Get your gear, Kade."

When Kade stepped back, Flinn laughed mockingly. "If you keep taking orders from your warriors you won't get anywhere. I told you a reject wasn't going to help you get ahead."

"And yet which one of us held the Pliethin?" Kade strode past Flinn and onto the verandah where he grabbed his gear.

"You've still got to manage a year without drawing excess attention to yourself. You're not gonna make it. With the risks you take it won't be a Knight who discovers you. It'll be a human who doesn't even know dragons exist."

"Leave him be, Flinn," Maira snapped.

Flinn faced Maira. "Stay out of my business."

"Then stay out of mine." Maira strode back to Amber's side, taking her arm. "Let's go. The company around this place sucks."

"Don't think about it," Kade warned Flinn.

"Then discipline your people when they deserve it. Just remember, your warriors are dispensable. No one would care if they disappeared. And unless you're planning on living as a renegade, no one will tolerate their behaviour."

Kade ignored Flinn, striding to the middle of the yard where Maira had taken Amber. Brann joined him and they both turned into dragons. Maira strapped the gear onto Brann and a leather saddle on Kade.

Amber stared at the saddle. "I guess that's my surprise." She sent a daggered look towards Flinn for having ruined the moment.

"Answer me, Kade! I know you can hear my thoughts." Flinn strode across the yard.

"Ignore him," Maira muttered to Amber. "Get in the saddle and let's get out of here." When Amber was in the saddle, Maira showed her how to strap herself in.

"Kade!" Flinn roared.

"Are you right up there?" Maira looked up at her.

Amber nodded, sending a cautious glance towards Flinn who came closer. Her legs automatically tightened as Kade leapt into the air, his wings snapping out. Maira and Brann followed them. Flinn bellowed in anger and threw himself at them, becoming a dragon as he did.

Amber didn't think. She reacted. Two balls of flame arrowed towards Flinn, impacting with his chest. He spiralled towards the ground, managing to get his wings pumping again at the last second. He streaked after them.

"You idiot!" Kade yelled at Amber.

"He attacked first. You're the one who's been making me practice."

"Car coming this way," Maira broadcast the words.

"My mum," Amber muttered when she spotted the car. They rose higher.

"Tell me how you did it. What is she?" Flinn broadcasted as he followed.

"None of your business."

"Then I'll let the Elders know."

"Kade-"

"It's an empty threat, Amber. He doesn't want anyone else to have the knowledge." Kade flew even higher.

"There's other things I can do to make your life difficult." Flinn flew beside them. *"Let's start with what*

I'll have my people tell your mother. She's knocking on the front door now."

Amber started to protest. She reined in her words at the last second. *"It doesn't matter, I'm grounded for life anyway. And it's not going to make me talk."*

"Name your price," Flinn ordered.

Amber laughed. Less than a month ago she'd been mildly popular. Now she had people throwing riches at her feet and giving her open ended offers, hounding her like she was some sort of celebrity. This wasn't her life. *"Get over it. You haven't got anything I want."*

"What about your mother? My people can ransom her back to you."

She battled the anger that rushed through her. They better not touch her mother. *"Guess that'll mean you won't be able to stay here for a year either. What happens if you fail, Flinn?"*

"Amber, quit tormenting him."

"But it's so much fun." Amber made herself laugh, trying to ignore the anger that bubbled under the surface. Her laugh turned into a squeal as Kade tilted sharply to the right. "Behave." She slapped her palm against his scales.

"Leave us alone, Flinn. We'll be back Sunday night."

Kade righted himself. *"I'll discuss it then. Providing you leave Amber's mother alone and tell her nothing."*

"I'll expect the truth or I'm taking this to the Elders."

"You should know by now that threats don't work with me. They only make me more determined," Kade warned.

Flinn didn't bother answering. He turned in mid-flight and headed back towards the house.

Amber ran her hand lightly over the spot she'd hit. *"I'm sorry. I didn't mean to let him know."* She sent her thoughts to Kade only.

"I know. We've got a couple of days to figure out how to deal with this. Forget it for now. How about we enjoy this camping trip?"

"We better since I'm going to be grounded for the rest of my life. I hope it's going to be worth it."

"Human parents are very limiting."

"You have no idea." Amber looked around her, surprised to find they were above a river. *"Where are we going?"*

"Somewhere secluded."

Chapter Sixteen

Amber took sunglasses from her backpack style handbag and slipped them on. The wind was making her eyes water. She looked at her phone. It took a few minutes for her to decide. Turning it on, she rang her brother's mobile phone the moment she saw she had coverage.

"What do you think you're doing? Dad and Mum are yelling at each other."

Like that was anything new. Not! "I need to get away for the weekend. Do you think you can convince them not to ground me for life?"

Jasper laughed sharply. "You've got to be kidding. They'll lock you up and throw away the key. They said you aren't to see those kids you've been hanging out with lately."

"They lied to me. They got me to move to Grandma's place under false pretences. I hate living there." She still couldn't believe her parents had done that to her.

"So? That doesn't mean you can take off for the weekend. Where are you going? Who are you with and what are you doing?"

"Oh stop it. You're starting to sound like Mum."

"Yeah, well I've had to listen to them yell since you took off."

"It hasn't been that long."

"More than ten minutes would have been too long. And Dad had the phone on speaker since she was too loud to have the phone to his ear. You don't know these kids. You're mad taking off into the bush with them."

"Probably."

"I know I complain about having a sister sometimes, but I don't want you to do something about my complaints."

Amber laughed. "I'm not suicidal if that's what you're worried about."

"Reckless can be just as bad."

"Jay-"

"Forget this trip and come home. I bet I could talk them into reducing the sentence if you did."

"No."

"Amber, don't be-"

"You call me stupid one more time and I'm going to email you the worst virus I can find."

"What did you expect me to say when you rang?"

"I wanted to know what was happening."

"Mum was talking about calling the cops."

"No!" She didn't want their weekend to ruin Kade's need to keep a low profile and risk him being discovered.

"Dad talked her out of it. He said there wasn't much they could do since you went of your own free will. You did, didn't you?"

"Yeah."

"Dad wants to talk to you."

"He's with you?"

"He is now."

"Tell him I hate being lied to. And I'm not staying in Hicksville for the rest of my life and I'll have who I want for my friends. I'm not spending the rest of my life grounded. I'm nearly seventeen."

"I don't think those comments are what they're wanting to hear."

"Amber!"

She cringed at the tone of her father's voice. "Yeah?"

"What do you think you're doing?"

"Going camping."

"What brought all this on?"

"At least I didn't lie to you about it. I could have easily put together an elaborate plan to make you think I was somewhere more acceptable for the weekend." The silence dragged out and Amber was tempted to fill it. She managed to control herself. It was one of her father's favourite techniques.

"Your mother says you're getting more unmanageable lately."

"How about I'm getting sick of being lied to."

"We knew you wouldn't have moved if it was to be longer than a school term."

"And that makes it right? How many times have you lectured me about telling the truth? And yet it's fine for both of you to lie to me? What were you going to do? Wait until the end of term and then tell me?"

"Your mother's on the home line. She wants to ring you."

"I don't want to talk to her yet. You can tell her I'll stay at Grandma's for the rest of the year without complaint if I can hang out with who I want, go wherever I want and come home when I want. I'll even make sure I keep up with my schoolwork. I'll give her destination and ETA. But if you expect me to be stuck in that town, there's got to be some sort of compensation."

"Don't be ridiculous, Amber."

"I'm not. That's my terms and they're not negotiable." The phone crackled. "Sounds like I'm about to lose coverage. I'll talk to you later."

"Amber, if you come home now, we'll sit down and discuss these issues-" The phone call dropped out.

Amber sighed heavily, turned her phone off and put it away. She was torn. She wanted to return home. To get back to her normal life. But that'd mean leaving Kade, Maira and Brann. She rested her palm against the scales on Kade's back, spreading out her fingers so she could touch as many of them as possible.

"Are you okay?"

She placed her other hand flat against his scales before she answered him. *"I guess."*

"Not bothered by the height?"

"Nah."

"Going too fast for you?"

"Fast? This turtle pace?"

"Any loose objects?"

"All secure. Why?"

"See the loops at the front of the saddle?"

Amber looked down. She ran her fingers over the

two braided pieces of leather attached on either side of the front of the saddle. *"Yep."*

"Put your arms through them and lean against me."

"Why?" Amber did as she was directed.

"I'll show you turtle pace!" Kade shot forward, spiralling as he did.

Amber's scream turned into laughter. *"Turtle!"*

Kade roared and sped up. Maira and Brann were left behind.

Amber threw her head back, wishing she could sit up, arms outstretched like she did on a roller coaster. "Yes!" The ground below them was a blur. The wind rushed at her and tangled her hair so it streamed behind her. The hair band that held it, snapped. Amber laughed again, giving herself over to sensation, ignoring all her problems.

At dusk Kade landed in a clearing near a creek. Amber helped him out of the saddle and he became human again. Dropping her handbag onto his saddle, she turned to face him. She couldn't stop grinning.

"Liked that ride, did you?" Kade grinned back at her.

"A saddle is much better than a harness."

"Because it keeps your hands free when we're not going fast?"

Amber groaned. "I apologised about the fireballs."

"Don't worry about it. At least it answered a question I had."

"Why would I need to throw fireballs while I'm on you?" Amber's eyes narrowed as she recalled Ronan's questions. "Is your clan going to war?"

"There's always someone at war. I was mainly thinking about wyverns, as well as Ronan and his people."

"But it doesn't help. The fireballs don't stop them. Well, they scared off the wyvern that was on its own."

"You have to aim for the wings."

"They move heaps! How am I meant to hit them?"

"Only do that if you want to cause long-term damage."

"The wings."

Kade nodded. "Yeah. The membranes between the veins can catch fire. A bit like if someone threw fire at your hair. It takes a while for them to grow back."

Amber's hand went automatically to her hair that was full of tangles from the wind. "What if they're airborne? Like really high."

"What do you think?"

"They'd die?" Amber's voice was a whisper.

Kade nodded.

"You want me to kill?"

"No need to shriek."

"You want me to kill!"

"Survival of the fittest. If it's between you and Ronan surviving, who would you choose?"

"He wouldn't kill me. He needs me alive for his schemes."

"What if it was between me and Ronan? He has no reason to keep me alive."

Amber's mouth dried and she stepped forward, a hand reaching out to rest on Kade's bare chest. "He's not killing you. I definitely wouldn't help him then."

Maira and Brann landed near them. Maira became human and unloaded the gear off Brann. "Thanks for sticking around."

Amber laughed at Maira's dry tone. "He was showing off because I called him a turtle."

Maira rolled her eyes. "Males." She snorted. "Males with egos!"

Brann changed into a human the moment the last of the gear was off him. "He has an unfair advantage. I don't have any Gold in my bloodlines. I bet you wouldn't do so well against your blood brother."

"Blood brother?" Amber asked.

Kade smiled. "Same as the meaning of brother for you."

"You have siblings?"

"You don't think my parents have produced only one offspring in the past century, do you?"

"Century."

Kade laughed. "No need to look so shocked. You already knew we lived for a long time."

"But they're still having kids. They're ancient and they're still having kids."

Kade turned to Maira and Brann. "Set up camp. We're taking a walk." He took Amber's hand and led her to the creek, following it upstream.

"Why do I feel like I'm not going to like what you've got to say?"

"Have you ever thought about why there are so many stories about Knights hunting dragons?"

Amber stopped abruptly. "They aren't myths?"

"Do I look like a myth?"

"Yes but… I mean the stories… knights and…" Amber shook her head. "Why did they?"

"Dragon blood was called the elixir of life."

"The… no!" She took a step back from Kade. She'd consumed the elixir of life? What the hell did that mean for her?

Kade reached out to her. "Amber, I'm s-"

She pushed his hand away. "No. I don't want to hear it. All I want you to say is, 'I've found a way to fix the problem.' You can keep all your sorry comments to yourself."

"I don't believe this problem can be fixed. The changes Pliethins cause in Gold Dragons are permanent."

"You never told me what changes it causes in dragons."

"No, I haven't."

"Fine! Then I don't have to tell you anything." Amber turned and started back for the camp. She didn't know whether to be glad or annoyed she could see in the dark so she didn't stumble over anything on the way back. Being able to see in the dark didn't change the fact that she wasn't human anymore. She didn't know what she was.

Kade put his hand on her shoulder and tried to get her to face him. She shrugged him away. "Amber, be reasonable."

"No. You aren't, so why should I? You're full of secrets. You hint at things and leave me wondering. Well, you can see exactly what it feels like to put up with that."

"We'll see if you feel the same way if my cousin comes across any information."

Anger coursed through Amber. Her hands became

fists. "Ronan would be willing to answer any question I ask him."

Kade grasped her by the shoulders, refusing to let her shrug him off. He forced her to face him. "You will stay away from him."

"I'm not one of your people."

"I wouldn't have been stupid enough to choose you."

Amber refused to let him see how those words hurt. She tried to pull away from him. He held her too tight. She did the only thing possible. She became a panther, leaping away from him, streaking through the bush, ignoring the direction of camp. In this form she could easily find her way back. She sensed Kade behind her, trying to force her to listen to his thoughts. She pushed his mind away, running faster.

The ground was a blur, made of places to step and places to avoid. Gum trees and shrubs rushed past her in the dark. Scents bombarded her. Tantalising scents as the night brought out the creatures that avoided the heat of the day. Suddenly Kade was above her, skimming as low as possible through the trees. Ahead was open ground. Amber veered off, aiming for thicker scrub. As she did, a startled hare leapt out in front of her.

Instinct took over and she pounced. The hare was

caught mid-stride and her momentum carried her forward. She came to a stop, dropping the limp body onto the ground. Hunching over her kill, her senses were alert for any who'd steal it.

"Amber." Kade walked slowly towards her, hands held open in a gesture of peace. He stopped when she growled. "Equal exchange of information."

Amber shook her head and growled.

"What do you want then?" Kade took another step forward.

Amber crouched, ready to spring forward.

"Run!" Maira's words screamed through their minds. An image of Brann pinned on the ground, while Ronan stood over him, followed the words. One of the people holding Brann down struggled to put grey metal chains on him.

Amber snarled, leaping past Kade. She raced for the campsite, the hare left bleeding on the ground. Kade flew after her.

"Amber! No! Don't go back there. You can't help them. Stop!"

All she could think of were the words Flinn had spoken earlier. 'Warriors are dispensable.' Kade hadn't corrected him. Well they weren't. She wasn't letting them be harmed because she could throw some stupid fireballs.

"Amber, I know you're in the area," Ronan broadcast.

She slowed as she came close to the camp.

Kade dropped down ahead of her, becoming human. "Don't do this. We'll get them back."

Chapter Seventeen

Amber leapt past him. She slowed to a stop as she reached the trees before the campsite, forcing the panther to retreat. Running the back of her hand across her mouth, she was surprised at the blood on her face. "Let him go." She could see Brann on the ground. He was a dragon, his front limbs chained. Ronan wasn't in sight. Two other men were.

"It's not up to me. You'll have to wait until Ronan comes back." The man who spoke had dark hair and his chest and upper arms were covered in a swirl of black tattoos.

Amber opened her mouth to speak. A blade at her throat stopped her words, an arm around her chest pinned her arms to her side.

"Surprise, surprise." Ronan's mouth was at her ear.

The scent of him surrounded her. Until that second, she hadn't smelt him or even felt his mind.

The blade was cold and sharp. She stayed perfectly still. "What do you want?"

"We tried to do it the easy way. I guess you prefer the hard way. Now move." Ronan pressed against her back so she was forced to walk into the clearing.

Amber's gaze met Brann's. She tried to reach out to his mind and talk to him. It was as if he wasn't there. Panic filled her as she wondered what they'd done to him. Was it permanent?

"Come out Kiani's boy. I have your mage and one of your people."

Kade entered the clearing from the other side of the campsite. "It's Kade. I left my parent's home years ago."

"Give yourself up or I'll kill your mage."

"He's bluffing. He needs me," Amber called. She stopped breathing when the blade pressed harder. She felt a trickle run down her throat. Sweat or blood, she wasn't sure.

Ronan laughed. "There's still a lot of harm I can do without actually killing you, mage."

"What will giving myself up do? It won't get her released." Kade took another step into the campsite.

"You can all go free once I have my lands back."

"I have to be home by Sunday night." Amber nearly groaned at making such a stupid comment.

"Think again, mage. It'll take longer than that just to do the planning."

"Stop calling me mage. My name's Amber."

"Quit stalling. There's no help coming. The other dragon's still in the area. I can smell her. And no calls for help have gone out. I've made sure of that. Now give yourself up before I kill your warrior over there."

Brann faced towards Kade, pressing himself to the ground. He closed his eyes.

"Get him up!" Ronan roared. "Now!"

The two men kicked at Brann but he didn't budge. Amber winced at every blow. Brann remained as still as stone even though it must have hurt. She saw him tense with each blow.

"Stop it! Leave him be!" If there hadn't been a blade against her throat she would have been across the clearing and dealing with Ronan's warriors.

"It looks like it bothers one of you at least." Ronan laughed. His grip loosened slightly.

Amber used that lapse to become a panther, turning on Ronan, claws and teeth sinking into him. The knife dropped to the ground. Ronan changed into a dragon. Claws skittered across scales and Amber leapt back warily. Ronan came for her again, his mouth open in a roar, his claws outstretched.

She leapt out of the way, spinning to face him as

he came at her again. Out of the corner of her eye she saw Kade take flight. She knew he wasn't as large as Ronan. She didn't know how he'd fare, but didn't think it'd be good. She turned human, hands raised, balls of fire aimed at the wings. Ronan was forced to dodge. Kade retreated.

"Amber!" Kade's warning came too late.

Amber landed face first in the dirt. Two bodies pressed her down. She struggled, getting a glimpse of tattoos. She'd forgotten about the two warriors guarding Brann. All her attention had been focused on Ronan. They flipped her onto her back, one of them holding chains similar to those on Brann.

"They're to deaden dragon power. Don't panic when you can't hear me," Kade warned. *"And Amber, I didn't mean what I said before. I was angry. I would choose you."*

The shackles snapped over her wrists, the chains between them dragged at her. She struggled to her feet the moment the men let her go. She didn't feel any different. She reached out towards Kade with her mind, careful to avoid Ronan. *"Can you hear me?"*

"Yes. Keep it to yourself though. And don't change while you're chained. We can use this."

"How?"

"I don't know yet."

Ronan came to stand in front of her. "Call your

dragon over mage. Or I'll kill the warrior, regardless of his offer to die, and then I'll start on you. Toes are only needed if you plan on walking."

Amber forced herself not to throw fire at him. She could feel every one of her toes in the boots Brann had made for her. She glanced first at Kade and then at Brann before her gaze returned to Ronan. She didn't know what to do.

"There's no need for that. I submit." Kade walked forward, his hands outstretched. He shook his head when Amber opened her mouth to protest. *"You have to get away as soon as you can. Don't worry about the rest of us. Escape. Ask Flinn to tell my clan. Tell him it will be my brother favour."*

Amber watched as chains were put on Kade. He instantly became a dragon and she could no longer sense him. She tried to run towards him. Ronan stepped in front of her.

"Call the other one in. Tell her if she wants her Gold Warrior to live she better come immediately."

Maira stepped out of the trees, her hands held out the same as Kade's had been. "I'm here."

Amber fought back tears as Maira was chained. She refused to cry. It did nothing. She wasn't weak. She had to figure out a way to escape this. A way for them all to get away, not just her. As if he knew what she thought, Kade lay on the ground facing her, eyes closed. She tried to yell no at him, but it was like he wasn't there. She clenched her teeth together. He wasn't going to do this. She wouldn't let him.

"You'll ride on Tory." Ronan pointed to the man with the tattoos.

"Who's the other one?" Amber looked at the man with the shaved head.

"Hound."

"I have a saddle for Tory to wear. Unless of course you want to risk me dying when I fall off him." Amber pointed towards the saddle, her handbag on the ground beside it.

"Tory. Change. Let the mage saddle you."

Tory shot her a look of disgust before he moved to stand beside the saddle and became a dragon. Amber walked over, picked up her bag and the saddle and threw it over him. She stepped around to the other side of him and pulled her mobile phone out, slipping it into the single pocket of her pants. It was difficult to do up the saddle with her hands chained together, but at least she was able to move them further apart than handcuffs would have allowed.

"What about my backpack? I can't live in the same clothes non-stop." Amber pointed to the item near one of the tents that had been set up.

Ronan strode over and opened it up. He rummaged through her stuff then handed the bag to her. He pointed to her handbag, holding out his hand. Amber reluctantly gave it to him. It came in for the same scrutiny before he handed it back. She shoved it inside her backpack and closed it. She would have liked to have worn it properly, but that was impossible with the chains.

Kade snorted and Amber looked over at him. He shook his head then stared at her. She smiled, almost able to see him telling her not to be stupid. She raised her chin. She didn't know how long it'd take her to escape, but she wasn't going days in the same clothes. Let him complain as much as he wanted. He shook his head again and his tail flicked back and forth. Those chains looked like they might be handy to have around sometimes. She glanced down at them and then returned her gaze to Kade's eyes. He snorted as if he knew exactly what she thought.

Ronan stepped between them. "What's going on?"

"He's annoyed with me for some reason. It's your fault I don't know why." Her hands went to her hips, the chain tight across her stomach.

"Too bad. Get on Tory. I want to be home before dawn."

The ride to Ronan's home was nothing like the

ride to the campsite. There was no excitement, no playing. She held the backpack on her lap, the strap over one of her arms as she held onto the leather loops at the front of the saddle. Leaning forward, she closed her eyes so she didn't have to watch her three friends fly nearby, their front paws chained together. They might be able to fly, but there was no point in them trying to escape without a means to remove the chains that stole their powers from them. They had no way of communicating and would be unable to fight.

Hours later, Amber opened her eyes as they started to descend. She caught a glimpse of Brisbane spread out below before she was amongst it. They landed in an industrial area. There were few lights, many windowless buildings and no traffic. She wondered if that changed at dawn.

Hound became human, pulled a key from his pants and unlocked a padlock. He swung open a large metal door and they all followed Ronan in. Amber dismounted as Hound shut the door behind them. When she removed the saddle, Kade snorted and she looked over at him. He lay on the ground and looked from the saddle to his back. Amber walked over to put it on him.

"What do you think you're doing?" Ronan grabbed her by the arm.

"I'm not about to carry it around." Amber gestured towards Kade. "He's stuck as a dragon so I might as well put it on him until I need to use it again."

Ronan stared at her a moment longer before he turned to Hound. "Lock up and get this lot in the back room." He strode to a set of stairs on the right side of the large open room.

Amber finished doing up the saddle before she looked around. The floor was stained concrete, the walls metal and the underneath of the roof was visible through the metal rafters. At the end of the room was another large metal door. Stairs at the side of the room were the only other exit.

"You heard him. Get in the back room." Tory gestured towards the metal door. He walked ahead of them, swinging it open.

The same stained floor, open rafters and metal walls greeted them. There were no lights and no windows. The door swung shut the moment they were all in the room. Amber heard the click of a padlock closing. Ignoring the sensation that caused in her stomach, she turned to Kade, throwing her arms around him. The chain caught between them. He rested his head on her shoulder for a moment before he pulled back. He stared at her. His tail flicked back and forth then he pushed her away with his head.

"Okay, I know what you're saying. Give me a break," Amber said irritably.

Kade head butted her again.

"Will you stop that? You're not the only one who can get stubborn when being ordered around and threatened." She stepped further into the room and froze. She felt a hum in the air. "Pliethin," she murmured. It couldn't be anything else. She looked around. It came from the direction the steps had led to. She crossed the room and placed her hands against the metal wall. The hum increased. She could feel the energy. She turned back to Kade. "Do you feel it?" She frowned when he shook his head.

Kade rose on his hind legs, holding up his chained paws.

"Oh. Okay." Amber pulled out her phone and turned it on. Ignoring the snort from Kade, she set it to vibrate mode and put all the other sounds to off or vibrate. That done, she checked her coverage. Perfect. Slipping it back into her pocket, she turned her attention to the chains. There was a keyhole on each shackle. Kade snorted again. Amber looked over at him. "You know, that sound's getting really annoying. Can any key open these or is it a special key? Or can they be cut off? And don't flick your tail at me. If you'd given me all the information you knew I wouldn't be working blind here."

Kade nodded and then shook his head.

"Right. Yes and no questions. Can any key open these chains? No? Okay. So I take it that means a special key."

Kade nodded. At the side of the room Maira paced. Brann lay on the ground. Amber frowned as she noticed how little he moved. Had they hurt him that bad when they were kicking him earlier? She ignored Kade's snort, walking over to Brann. He flinched when she rested her hands on him.

"I'm sorry," Amber whispered.

Brann shook his head slightly, tensing at the movement.

"Stay still." Amber felt the energy build in her hands. Surely there must be something she could do. If she could fuse skin together then other healing must be possible. She didn't know what was wrong and it wasn't like she could x-ray him. She smiled wryly as she wondered if you could get an x-ray machine large enough. Maybe one suitable for an elephant. Kade snorted behind her again. "Oh shut up, Kade." Would she make things worse if she poured some of the healing energy into him?

"Brann, I don't know what I can do, or if I'll make it worse. I don't even know what's wrong. But I could try and help. Are you willing to let me?" When Brann nodded, Amber closed her eyes. She felt the energy build up. It was like pin pricks against her palms. She focused on healing and wholeness. She didn't know what else to think of. She let the energy go. She bit her lip at the sudden flare of pain in her palms. Brann recoiled. Her eyes opened to see blue points of light dance across the chain between his paws. Healing and wholeness? Had she just tried to cure the communication problem?

A wave of exhaustion washed over Amber and she sat on the ground before her legs gave out. That hadn't happened last time. Kade nudged her back and she turned to face him, pressing her palm against his head. Brann nudged her shoulder and she looked at him. He stood. He raised his head and then dipped it, his body pressing against the ground. Amber had the impression of being bowed to.

"Did that help?" She grinned when Brann nodded. Her grin faded when Kade nudged her again. "Oh, stop being so impatient. I'm thinking." She thought it was best not to tell him she'd probably overdone things by healing Brann. "I forgot to ask, is there any way of getting these chains off without a key?"

Amber frowned when Kade shook his head and then nodded. "Well, that wasn't helpful." She rose shakily to her feet as her phone vibrated. It was a text message from Crystal.

Did you go camping to get out of having me visit?

She returned her phone to her pocket. She'd talk to Crystal later. Right now she had to find out where she was. She wished she knew someone who could track her down by using her mobile phone. Obviously she didn't know the right kind of people. Or she was hanging out with the wrong kind. She glanced between the three dragons then stared at Kade.

Chapter Eighteen

"Does Flinn have a phone I can reach him on?" Amber swore when Kade shook his head. There went that plan. She sat down again. Kade nudged her and she swatted at him. She couldn't ring her brother. She didn't have the time to convince him not to tell their parents. Crystal and Angela were both still sixteen and had no transport. "Stop pushing me!" She glared at Kade again. He glared back. "Ten minutes. Give me ten minutes to think."

When Kade nodded, Amber closed her eyes. She had to figure out where they were. She reached out with her mind. There were people on the street outside now. Grinning as she realised she could sense all of them, she ranged further away. She wondered where Crystal was. She felt a tug from one of the directions. She followed it, picturing Crystal as she did. She tried to focus on the direction she took. It was difficult. Then she found her. She almost shouted in excitement, but managed to hold back. Now maybe she could find Flinn.

She searched out in the direction she thought Hicksville was in. The sensation of people grew weaker. Eventually she could sense nothing. Next plan. She thought of the handful of people she knew in Hicksville. Her mother and grandmother, both not an option. Jessica and Justin Chambers. Not the best of options, but at least a chance. She dialled the operator and asked for their home number. Seconds later she was ringing their house, butterflies diving in her stomach.

"Yeah?"

"Jessica?"

"Yeah? Who's this?"

"It's Amber. Kade asked me to ring you. He's trying to get a message to Flinn."

"Tell him I'm not a messenger."

"He really needs someone to take a message to Flinn and get him to ring back on this phone."

"So? Not my problem. Bye."

"Wait!"

"What?"

"Is Justin there?"

"No." The phone clunked down.

Amber swore. She wanted to strangle Jessica. She needed to figure out another plan. When Kade nudged her again, she swatted him. His answer was to nudge her harder. "Give me a break. I'm trying here."

Maira pounced in front of them. She looked back and forth between Amber and the door. Amber heard the sound of the padlock being opened and quickly shoved her phone in her pocket.

"Brann, lie down again," she hissed before the door swung open.

Hound threw a dead kangaroo into the room. "You can't say we don't look after you." He smirked.

Amber rose to her feet. "I can't eat raw meat."

Hound shrugged. "Not my problem. Anyway, Ronan wants to see you. Move it."

Kade moved in front of her when she took a step forward. She rested her hand against him. "I'll be back shortly." His tail flicked back and forth as she walked away from him. She stared at the three of them as the door swung shut and the padlock was slipped into place again. Her gaze was drawn to the door at the other end, which was now padlocked from the inside.

Hound pointed towards the stairs. "Don't have all day."

As if reminded of her lack of sleep, Amber yawned. She walked towards the steps, conscious of Hound behind her. The door at the top of the stairs was a flimsy wooden one. It opened into a room with sturdy, medium brown carpet on the floor. A black leather lounge suite was gathered around a timber coffee table in the middle of the room and the walls were lined and painted an off white. There were no windows, only two doors on the opposite wall.

Ronan was sprawled in one of the armchairs. When Amber entered he gestured to the one across from him. "Take a seat, mage. We have things to discuss."

Amber sat on the edge of the chair, her gaze drawn to a carved wooden box in the centre of the coffee table. The air crackled with the energy coming from the box. "Your decorating skills are a bit on the bare side." Her gaze travelled around the empty walls. She wanted to draw his attention away from how long she'd stared at the box. Why did he have a Pliethin?

Ronan shrugged. "We never stay anywhere long. It's best not to draw attention to ourselves. Can I get you something? A drink? Food?"

"Pizza." She hoped deliveries counted as attention they didn't want.

Ronan pulled a wallet from his pants, drew out some money and waved it towards Hound. "You heard her."

"But–"

Ronan sat up straight. "Never argue with me."

Hound nodded, took the money and left the room. Ronan tossed his wallet on the coffee table and leaned back again.

"You're hard on your people."

"Sons."

"And I thought my parents sucked."

Ronan laughed. Then he grew serious. "Can you heal? Is that one of your abilities?"

Amber shook her head. She didn't plan to share any more information than necessary with him. "Why?"

"Your dragons damaged one of my sons. He'll be out of action for at least a month. So what abilities do you have?"

"The fireballs aren't enough for you?"

"Don't take me for a fool. I've known several mages before. And they've always had more than two abilities."

"What happened to the mages you knew?"

"You mages are more frail than us dragons. I've only known one that didn't die in battle. He even outlived his dragon by about a decade. But he was a bit younger than the dragon and one of his abilities was shielding himself. Now, back to the original question, what are your abilities?"

At least now she could stop worrying that she might die if Kade did. "If you let some of my friends go I'd be more cooperative."

Ronan laughed mirthlessly. "Don't take me for an idiot, mage." He rose to his feet. "I'll take you back to your friends." He spoke the last word like it was something disgusting. "Maybe spending some time with them will remind you of what you will lose if you don't follow orders."

Amber rose to her feet, walking towards the door without urging. She managed to keep her gaze off the carved box. She didn't want to alert him to her interest. The trip downstairs was made in silence. Ronan took a key from his leather pants and unlocked the padlock. He pulled the door open enough for Amber to slip in.

"Hound will bring you your food when he returns. Cooperate and we'll make life easier for you. There's no need for you to spend your time in this room." Ronan pushed the door closed and locked it.

Amber stared at the door a moment longer. A nudge at her back drew her attention. She turned to see Kade. She had to come up with a plan now. Hound was gone, but she didn't know for how long. There was an injured dragon upstairs, which was probably why Ronan only had two dragons with him this time and she guessed Tory wasn't about or Ronan wouldn't have taken her back to the room. He didn't seem the type to do the drudgework.

Her nose wrinkled. There was a strange smell in the room. She followed the scent to the kangaroo the dragons hadn't touched. "Don't eat that." She pointed to the carcass. "There's something wrong with it." The dragons dipped their heads. Satisfied they'd leave it alone, she pulled her phone out, dialling Crystal's number. "Are you alone?"

"How about letting me get in a hello?"

"No time. Remember I told you about a life and death situation? Well, we need your help." As she spoke, Amber reached out with her mind to find Crystal. This time it was easier. "Stay still."

"What?" Crystal's voice was shrill.

"Hey! My eardrums."

"You can see me?"

"No. Now take five steps in one direction. No, wrong one. Try a different direction. Nope, the opposite one."

"What the hell is going on?"

"Stop asking questions. There's an industrial estate in that direction. Take note of the direction. Ring Jay. Tell him I'm in really bad trouble and he's not to tell our parents. Tell him I'm not joking and it's extremely important he doesn't tell anyone."

"You're scaring me, Amber."

"Good, because I'm terrified too."

"You don't sound it."

"Do I ever?"

"No. That's me I guess."

"Hurry, Crys. Time's running out." She hung up. If anyone could convince her brother not to tell their parents, it was Crystal. Kade's tail flicked back and forth. She could almost feel the anger pour off him. She returned his glare. "Your mate isn't contactable. Mine is. Live with it. Ronan's got a Pliethin upstairs in a box. I can't reach Flinn with my mind. I don't know if I normally would be able to or if these chains make it hard." She frowned, eyeing the shackles that sat loosely around her wrists. Within seconds she was a panther and the chains slipped off her as she changed. As soon as she was human again, she tried to reach out to Flinn. It was no different. She didn't have that range.

She supposed the next step was to get out of here. Turning, she faced the door. How hot did metal have to be to melt? She guessed she was about to find out. Calling up a ball of fire, she increased the heat, holding it against the door where she thought the padlock was. Nothing. She increased the heat further. Sweat poured down her face and she stepped back, her arm outstretched as far as possible. The door began to twist and glow near the fireball. Amber wished she had something she could push through it. There was no way she was going to touch the hot metal with her hand. Just because the fire didn't hurt her didn't mean the metal wouldn't. She heard a pop as the latch, the padlock was on, let go of the door and a clatter as it hit the ground.

Closing her hand she extinguished the fire. She pushed the door open, the metal at the middle of the door hot against her palm. The room was empty. Relief hit her and she grabbed her backpack, pulling it on as she ran to the door. She pushed on it slightly. It wasn't locked. Turning, she found Kade next to her.

"Guard this door." She tried to head for the stairs, but he was in front of her. "I have to get that Pliethin." Kade shook his head violently. "Yes. Don't stand here arguing with me, or we'll get caught." She headed for the stairs again. She had no clue what she'd do with the Pliethin, but it was obviously valuable to dragons if the way Kade and Flinn had tried to get it was any indication. Halfway up the stairs, her phone started to vibrate. She checked the display. It was Crystal. "Yeah?"

"We think we know which industrial estate you're talking about. Anything else?" Crystal asked.

"Yeah. Tell Jay to hire the largest enclosed trailer he can." Amber waited for Crystal to pass along the message. She smiled as she heard her brother swear in the background.

"Okay. Anything else?"

Amber reached out with her mind. They were heading in the correct direction. "No. Just hurry."

"We are."

Amber hung up and slipped the phone back in her pocket, cautiously making her way up the rest of the steps. Reaching out with her mind, she checked the room. Finding only the Pliethin there, she eased the door open. All was clear. Dashing inside, she grabbed the carved box, hesitated, then grabbed the wallet too. She hoped there'd be enough money in there to pay her brother back. Hurrying down the stairs, she shoved the box and wallet in her backpack. The three dragons waited by the exit for her.

She peered outside. Vehicles were parked along the side of the street and people walked on the concrete footpaths. There was no way she could take three dragons outside. Not and keep them hidden. Panic rose up and she beat it back down, along with the panther that wanted to escape. There had to be a way. She could see freedom. It was centimetres away. Behind her Kade snorted. She turned back to him. His tail still moved back and forth in an angry cat fashion.

"I'm not leaving you here." She ignored his violent nod and turned back to the gap in the door. She reached out with her mind. Crystal and Jasper were still too far away. Amber stepped into the street. No one paid her any attention. She bet that'd soon change if one of the dragons followed her. Several doors away was another building locked up tight. Reaching in with her mind she found it was empty. That is if you didn't count the mice. Hurrying to the empty building, she kept her back to the handful of people nearby and called up another fireball.

This time she tried to keep it small and concentrated. The padlock popped open with the heat and Amber quickly removed it, dropping the hot metal on the ground, biting back a yelp when she touched it. She opened the door and kicked the padlock inside. Now she had to find something to cover them with. A quick scan of the room showed it was empty. She didn't have time to search the entire building.

Amber closed the door and slowly walked back towards where her friends were being held. Her gaze scanned the area and she spotted a painter's ute. A pile of drop cloths were folded and sitting in the back. The painter was standing at the front of his vehicle talking to someone.

A deep breath and she hurried over to him. "Excuse me."

The painter turned towards her, irritation on his face. He pulled his cap off, rubbed the sweat from his forehead and replaced it. "What?"

"I have some trolleys of stuff I need to move a few buildings along and I forgot to bring the covers. The stuff is light sensitive. I'm wondering if I could borrow your drop cloths. It shouldn't take me more than ten minutes."

"What is it?"

"Stuff belonging to the photographer who's working in that building." Amber pointed to where they'd been held. "I just can't afford to lose this job and I don't have enough time to return with the cloths before my boss gets back." She held her breath, hoping he'd say yes.

The painter sighed. "Need a hand with it?"

Amber shook her head. "No. Some of it's really fragile. I guess I'd better do it myself."

"Ten minutes. Then I've got to hit the road."

"Thank you." Amber couldn't resist a grin. She

walked to the back of the ute with the painter and was surprised at how heavy the two drop cloths were that he handed her. "I'll be as quick as possible." She hurried back to the building and slipped inside.

Chapter Nineteen

The three dragons stared at Amber. She was still grinning. Now if only her luck would hold a little longer. "Who's first? I need you to hold your tail on an angle suitable for the handle of a large trolley. I've got a building to hide you in until my brother can find us."

Kade pointed towards Maira, who shook her head.

"Quit arguing or I won't be able to get any of you out of here."

Maira stepped forward. Amber quickly draped the paint splattered cloths over her and then holding onto her tail, waited until Kade nudged the door open further before pushing against Maira's tail.

"Go in the opposite direction of where I move your tail, unless I'm pushing forward," Amber whispered. "Just like a trolley." She stopped talking as she stepped out into the light and held her breath as they moved slowly along. The slight breeze that ruffled the drop cloths masked the walking motion and she sped things up a little, pulling back on Maira's tail once they reached the building she'd broken into. Then she guided Maira in. As soon as they were inside, she pulled off the drop cloths, closed the door on Maira and rushed back to Kade and Brann.

With every minute that passed, Amber became more anxious. She had to stop herself from constantly looking around. Instead, she searched the area for dragons with her mind. It continued to stay clear. She didn't search Ronan's building since she didn't want to risk alerting anyone. She had no idea exactly how her abilities worked and if anyone would notice what she was doing. Once all three dragons were hidden she returned the drop cloths and grabbed the chain from their cell. Shoving it in her backpack, she shut the door behind her and left Ronan's building for what she hoped was the last time.

Taking note of the number on the front of the building, she stepped inside with her friends. She stopped in front of Kade. "Ronan can't find your minds while you've got these chains on, can he?" Kade shook his head. "That's what I thought. You know I can't stay here with you, don't you?" Kade nodded. "Let Jay and Crystal help you, please. Let them get you out of here." She pulled out the wallet, her jaw dropping open when she saw all the fifty-dollar notes inside. She took several hundred out for herself and checked for ID. There was only the money. "Give this wallet to Jay. He can use it to help you escape." She couldn't resist smiling. "It seems fitting to me." She threw her arms around Kade. "Be careful."

Before she chickened out, Amber slipped outside and glanced around. There was still no sign of Ronan's warriors. She hurried down the street and hoped she wasn't heading in the direction they'd come from. Taking note of the name of the street as she turned the corner, she pulled her phone out.

"We've only just got a trailer now," Crystal said.

"Good. You'll need large cloths too. Like painter's drop cloths."

"How many?"

"Six should do."

"What are we picking up?"

There was no way she could explain it over the phone. It was something that needed to be seen to be believed. "I want you to keep an open mind and to ring me before you try to move the… ah… items."

"Where do we have to pick these items up from?"

Amber gave her the address. "Make sure you ring me first."

"Okay."

"And tell Jay I've left money there to help cover the cost of moving the… items."

"Aren't you there?"

"Not anymore."

"Amber-"

She spied a taxi and waved it down. "I have to go. Ring me when you arrive."

"Okay."

"Where to?" The taxi driver asked as she hopped in.

"Roma Street train station." She sat her backpack on her lap. Now that she could relax for a few minutes, her mind seemed frozen. She wasn't sure what to do next. Did she try and return home now? What if Ronan caught Jay and Crystal while they were trying to move the dragons? Then her mind went blank again. Sleep. That's what she really needed. She struggled to ignore her body's requirements. Her stomach rumbled and reminded her of another need. She might have better control over her panther, but it wasn't perfect. She needed food.

At the train station, Amber first used the bathroom and then grabbed a strong coffee and a sandwich.

Since she only had more dragon-leather in her backpack, she bought a shirt plastered with advertising to pull on over her leather vest and then studied what destinations were available to her. When her phone rang, she nearly dropped her coffee. The display read Crystal.

Amber answered the phone. "Have you arrived yet?"

"What the hell is going on?"

"Jay."

"Don't Jay me! There's… there's… shit!"

"Dragons?"

Jasper swore again.

Amber couldn't resist giggling.

"And money! There's a few grand here."

"Jay. Calm down."

"What the hell are you into? And why are they chained up? And why the hell does one of them keep glaring at me and slashing his tail around?"

"Ah, that'd probably be Kade. Tell him I'm safe." Amber waited while her brother repeated her words.

"Okay, that calmed him down a bit. Now what's going on?"

"We'll sort that out later. First, you have to get them out of there."

"They're not all going to fit in the furniture trailer

at once. I might be able to get two in. Why did Kade step back and push the other two towards me?"

Amber hurried over to a bench seat and dropped onto it. Her legs felt weak at the thought of Kade left there alone. She forced herself to concentrate. "He wants you to take them first."

"He can understand me?"

"Yeah." There was silence. Amber grew more worried. "Are you still there?"

"I had a spiked drink at the party I was at last night, didn't I?"

Amber smiled. She knew exactly how he felt. "If it makes you feel better to think that."

"Yeah, just peachy. So what do I do now?"

Amber reached out with her mind. The street was clear. She searched further. And there they were. Searching the streets for their escaped prisoners. She quickly pulled back. "Move them. Quickly. While the coast is clear."

"How do you know that?"

"Trust me. No time to explain yet."

"Where do you want me to take them?"

"Hicksville."

"It'll take me more than eight hours to get there and back."

It was Amber's turn to swear. "Leave two cloths and go."

"Amber."

"Hurry. Please. Question me later when we're all safe."

"Take care, Amber."

"I'm trying to." She hung up and stared at the phone. Now what? If she waited until they got the dragons home and she could ask Flinn to help, there'd be at least six hours before he could return to Kade. If he agreed to help. That was too long. Rising to her feet, she started walking, trying to stay awake. Sitting wasn't helping. If only she had a licence. And she didn't know anyone else with one.

Although she did know how to drive. Maybe... she shook her head. What if she was caught? Why would she be? It wasn't long before she'd be able to go for her provisional licence. But if she was caught... the better question would be, what if Kade was caught?

She rang Jasper's phone as she hurried towards the taxi rank. "I'll meet you somewhere."

"What?"

"I'll take your car. You can take the taxi I'm about to catch and go hire another vehicle and trailer."

"No. You don't have a license."

"That's the risk I have to take. Jay, if they're found, someone's going to kill them."

"Where are you?" When Amber told him, he quickly suggested a place to meet.

"I'll owe you big time."

"You better believe it."

Amber hurried to the taxi rank and hopped into the first one, giving the driver the destination Jasper had told her. She reached out with her mind. Ronan and his two dragons were headed in her direction. Not good. She forced herself to stay calm, to make the panther back down. Trying to take her mind off the situation, she focused on the handmade dreamcatcher hanging from the rear view mirror.

"What feathers are they?"

"Hawk. My daughter made it for me."

Amber stared at it thoughtfully. "Are you willing to sell it?"

"Well…"

"Fifty dollars."

"I don't know."

She really wanted those feathers. Wanted to see if she could use the Pliethin to alter what she could change into. "What's your price?"

"Eighty."

"Done." Amber pulled the money out, holding

back the grin that threatened to escape at the expression on the taxi driver's face.

He shoved the notes into the pocket of his shirt before he unhooked the dreamcatcher and handed it to her.

Amber put it inside her backpack. "Thanks."

He shrugged. "I guess at that price I can pay her to make me another one. She should get a buzz out of that."

They fell silent. Amber checked on Ronan again. She couldn't find him. But she could find his warriors. Could he hide himself? Is that why she hadn't noticed him before he put the knife to her throat? How were they meant to work around that? He could be anywhere.

"Have you got pen and paper I could use?"

The taxi driver handed over a notebook and pen. Amber tore a page out and rested it on the front cover. She did a quick sketch of Ronan. She frowned, then altered it slightly. It wasn't perfect, but it gave a fairly good impression of him. Nearly twelve years of doing art at school might have paid off after all. And her parents had always said it was a waste of time doing it as a subject in high school. She handed the pen and notebook back, slipping the picture into the front pocket of her backpack.

They arrived at the destination before Jasper and Crystal. Amber searched for Hound and Tory. They were still travelling towards her. She guessed they must be in a car. They weren't going fast enough to be flying. How long would it be before they decided to fly? As soon as they were away from the city? When it was dark? Was she going to lead them back to Kade's home?

"Are you getting out?" The driver asked.

"I'm waiting for someone." She handed over the money currently on the meter. "He'll need a lift somewhere."

"Okay."

Amber got out of the taxi as she sensed them getting closer. Then she spotted her brother's car, towing an enclosed trailer. They pulled over in front of the taxi.

Crystal was out of the car and running towards her before the engine was off. She threw her arms around Amber. "What have you got yourself into?"

Amber smiled. "Later. No time yet." She looked at her brother as he reached them. He handed over his keys. "Thanks."

"Be careful."

Amber nodded. "You too." She gave him the sketch she'd done. "Keep an eye out for this person.

I want you to arrive in one piece." She pulled away from Crystal to hug her brother, whose chin rested momentarily on her head, the colour of their hair blending. "Take really good care of Kade for me."

Jasper nodded, his blue eyes filled with a look of concern as he momentarily rested a hand on her shoulder then turned and walked to the taxi. Amber watched him go, his familiar slim form carried away by the taxi. She suppressed the urge to call out a warning, hurrying to the trailer instead.

Amber tapped twice on the side. "I'm driving now. Jay's going back for Kade." Her answer was two knocks.

Chapter Twenty

As soon as they were on the road, Crystal began with the questions. A steady stream of them that Amber had no hope of answering.

"Please," Amber begged.

"I have so much I need to know."

"You and me both. They're pretty stingy with their answers. All I can tell you is that yes, it is the Kade, Maira and Brann you met last weekend and normally they can change back into humans."

"Why can't they?"

"It's the chains."

"How did you find out about them?"

"It's a very complicated story."

"Are you going to tell me?"

"I basically stumbled onto their secret. Look, I can't tell you any more until I discuss it with Kade. He's really angry I brought you into the problem. But I couldn't leave them there. And I needed to find help for myself too. There's another dragon after me. One that's really old and has abilities Kade doesn't."

"If you're trying to scare me, it's working far too well."

Amber reached out and clasped Crystal's hand for a second before she put it back on the steering wheel. "I'm petrified of what he plans to do. It takes every bit of willpower to talk to him without turning to jelly. Are you sure you want to come with us? I can drop you somewhere and you can catch a taxi home. I'll pay for it."

"No. I might have nightmares for life, but I won't desert you."

"Trust me, you don't know what nightmares are until you dream of blood red eyes stalking you."

Crystal shuddered. "Great! Now I will."

Amber chuckled. "Sorry. I guess you will. You've never been able to watch horror movies." They fell into companionable silence.

The quiet was broken about half an hour later by Jasper ringing. Amber handed her phone to Crystal to answer.

"He's with Kade."

Amber reached out with her mind. The dragons were still following her. A little closer, but not by much. "Tell him to keep an eye out for the man in the picture. The others aren't there."

When Crystal finished passing on the message and ended the phone call, she asked, "So where are they?"

"Following us."

"What!"

"You still want to come with me?"

It took Crystal nearly a minute to answer. "I think so."

A few minutes later, the phone rang again. Jasper and Kade were on their way. Amber relaxed a little. They were safe for now. She glanced around at the thinning traffic. Not a good sign. A car passed her and she looked at her speedo. There was no way she could go any faster than eighty while towing. She hoped she came across someone slower than her that she could sit behind. The last thing she wanted was to be alone on the road in case Hound and Tory caught up to her.

By the time they pulled up at Kade's house, Amber was shaking with exhaustion. She dropped her head on the steering wheel, unable to move.

"Do you want me to let the dragons out?"

Amber could only answer Crystal with a nod. She needed sleep. Even an hour would be good. Instead, she forced herself to open the car door and stumble out. She grabbed her backpack and pulled it on. Her head jerked up as the front door swung open and Flinn strode out. He stared at her for a moment before he came towards her.

"What's going on? Who'd you bring with you? Where's Kade? Why can I sense a Pliethin and who are the dragons tailing you that tried to barge in on my mind?"

"We need help." She turned to see what Flinn laughed at. Maira and Brann stood behind her, Crystal behind them. "It's not funny."

"Oh yes it is. Maira more than anyone deserves it. She's always thought herself better than anyone else since one of her grandparents is Gold. Not enough to pass it along to her though. You ask any warrior. They'll all say the same. Almost Gold isn't good enough."

"Please help them." Amber hated having to beg Flinn. "Kade wants you to tell his clan. He said it'd be his brother favour." Crystal came to stand beside her.

"No. Not a brother favour. Not with the trouble you brought with you." He gestured skyward before he turned his attention to Crystal. "Who's this?"

"Crystal, this is Flinn."

"Don't you think enough humans already know about us?"

Amber shrugged. "She's my friend. She won't say anything."

"I'll help on two conditions."

"What?"

"You and the Pliethin."

"No!" Amber was echoed by Maira's roar.

"What's he mean by you?" Crystal asked.

Amber held out her hand. Fire appeared in it and she threw it up in the air like a ball. When it landed on her palm again, she snapped her hand shut and it disappeared.

Crystal's jaw dropped. She blinked. Finally, she managed to speak. "Show off."

Amber smiled slightly before she turned back to Flinn. "Try again. No deal."

"It's not negotiable. You don't know where to find someone to help. I'll call Kade's parents. All you have to do is answer to me instead of Kade and give me the Pliethin."

"I don't answer to Kade. You can even ask him that. You and I would kill each other within the space of a week. If that long."

"You and the Pliethin."

"How do you learn to do that?" Crystal asked. She reached out to touch Amber's palm. "Could I learn?"

"Sort of."

Crystal met Flinn's gaze. "Then what about me instead of Amber?"

"Crystal! No! You can't reverse the process if you don't like it."

"We've always done everything together. Why should this be any different? You're not leaving me out of it."

"I'd leave myself out of it if I could."

"Only because it takes you ages to get used to new things. Give it another month and you won't want it any different. It'll be normal for you. And don't bother arguing. I know you too well."

"He's a real pain to put up with. He expects everyone to follow orders."

Crystal grinned. "I guess he'll soon learn not everyone does."

Amber laughed, turning back to Flinn. "Well?"

"She will follow orders."

Amber shrugged. "We're only human."

"That isn't negotiable."

"Then no deal. You find some other way to get your Pliethin and Dragon Mage. I'll figure out another way to help Kade." She managed to control the smile that wanted to escape when Flinn growled.

"She will at least try and follow orders."

"She can hear you." Crystal glared at Flinn. "And she will only follow orders that are reasonable."

"You don't own her. Crystal will work with you for as long as you treat her well."

Flinn nodded sharply. "Let's get this over with." Flinn turned away and strode towards the back of the house.

Maira threw herself in front of Amber and Crystal when they started to follow. She growled with teeth bared.

"Back off, Maira. Kade isn't here to deal with this mess. And even if he was, he couldn't do any more than you can."

Maira forced Amber to take a step back. Amber let fire fill her hand.

"I will throw this and I will aim for the wings. Don't push me. I'm tired, exhausted and fed up with running from Ronan. I'm not in the mood for any more dramas." Amber stepped forward and Maira retreated. Brann growled from behind her. She turned to face him. He did the strange bow from earlier. Maira howled, outrage filling the sound. Amber turned back and Maira stepped out of the way, her tail flicking back and forth. Amber closed her hand and the fire went out. She hurried around the house, Crystal at her side.

Flinn waited, impatiently pacing. "Change your mind?"

Amber shook her head. "A slight disagreement. What's the quickest way for Gold Dragon blood to get into the body?"

"Into the blood stream through a cut or by drinking it."

Crystal screwed up her face. "I'm not drinking someone's blood."

One of Flinn's hands momentarily became a claw and he ran it across his palm. He held out the hand to Crystal.

"You never said anything about blood and cutting." Crystal stared at the blood pooling in Flinn's hand.

"Are you backing out already?" Flinn demanded. "If you won't drink it, a cut is the only other way."

Crystal glared at him and stepped forward, her hand outstretched. Her eyes closed at the last second so she didn't see the claw rake across her palm. She hissed when she felt it. Flinn pressed their palms together and Crystal tried to pull away. "It's burning!"

"It's meant to," Amber said.

"A warning would've been good."

Amber ignored her friend's glare. "I know you." She smiled. "You would've alternated between yes and no as you tried to psych yourself up. This way we did it without all the procrastinating."

Crystal rubbed her uncut hand across her arm. "Why does the air feel weird? Like it's full of energy."

"That's the Pliethin you can feel." Amber frowned. "Although it doesn't feel as strong to me as the last one did."

"That's because you've already used one," Flinn said.

When Crystal started to ask another question, Flinn interrupted her. "Now what?"

"You were there that night. I had the Pliethin for at least a minute, maybe two. Kade held me as both dragon and human while I held the Pliethin. I don't know if that makes a difference." She turned to Crystal. "No matter what happens, you can't let go of the Pliethin until Flinn takes it. That's extremely important."

"It's going to hurt, isn't it?"

"Yeah. But you have to take it the moment I give it to you or there mightn't be enough energy left in it for what he has to do. Okay?"

"Why are you giving it to her?" Flinn demanded.

"Because I want to check something out. And I was the one who got it."

"There better be enough energy," Flinn warned.

Amber ignored him and took the dreamcatcher out. She removed two of the feathers and handed one to Crystal. "Make sure you don't let go of the feather either." She held tightly to hers as she pulled the box out. Calling forth fire, she heated the padlock until it popped open. She unhooked the padlock, an indrawn breath at the heat on her fingers. Staring at her hand, she couldn't find a single blister from the heat. She guessed that was something, even if touching hot metal was painful.

"Hurry up," Flinn said.

Amber opened the box slightly and grabbed the Pliethin. The air crackled with energy and a jolt of it went through her arm. She turned to Crystal, handing it to her friend. Her teeth were clenched hard as she fought the wave of pain. Crystal clutched the Pliethin. Flinn was instantly there. He was a dragon for a minute, becoming human before he took the Pliethin Crystal struggled to hold onto. She staggered back the moment Flinn had the Pliethin. A ragged breath escaped her and Amber threw her arms around her friend.

"I could almost hate you for not warning me about how much pain that would be," Crystal whispered. "Oh my god."

Amber turned to see what Crystal looked at. Flinn

held the Pliethin, wings outstretched, forelimbs held in a victory type position, the Pliethin grasped tightly in one claw. And he blazed gold. The air around him shimmered with the colour.

"I want to reach out and touch him to see if he's real." Crystal's voice was an awed whisper.

"Don't. I'm not sure what that would do."

"Oh Amber, if this is a dream, I never want to wake up. How could you not want this?"

"Some moments are good, but there's a lot of moments that are mostly a nightmare." The crackle of energy in the air began to lessen. Amber continued to watch, an arm around Crystal's waist. Crystal had her arm around Amber and they leaned against each other. Amber yawned. She desperately needed sleep. But not until help arrived.

The glow around Flinn faded and he shimmered into human form, dropping to his knees. His gaze was focused on the Pliethin in his hand. The dull, misshapen creature lay there, unmoving.

Crystal cried out, kneeling in front of Flinn to gently touch the Pliethin.

"It will be fine," Flinn said softly. He raised his hand. "Thank you." As soon as he opened his hand the creature rose above it and faded away. Flinn looked over at Crystal's gasp. "It returned to its own world. It'll come back when it starts to regain energy."

"Are you sure it's okay?" Crystal asked.

Flinn could only nod. He looked too exhausted and dazed to do anything else. His head came up as they all heard a vehicle and he struggled to get to his feet. Amber came forward to help Crystal pull him up.

"It's okay. It's Jay and Kade."

"Who's Jay?" Flinn demanded.

"My brother."

"Another human?" Flinn didn't bother to keep the derision from his voice.

Amber smiled wryly. "Can you still call Crystal and me human?"

Flinn only grunted in answer.

The three of them walked towards the front yard and arrived in time to see Kade come out of the back of the trailer, his tail moving irately as he glared at them.

"Call for help," Amber told Flinn before she hurried to Kade. She threw her arms around him and refused to let him shake her off.

He hissed and finally managed to pull back. He sniffed at her then growled.

"Not being able to talk to you is really frustrating." She grabbed the chain and, remembering the energy that had played along Brann's, she pooled fire in her hand before she released it into the chain. Amber staggered, nearly hitting the ground. Jasper grabbed her in time. The world spun around and she took several deep breaths as she tried to bring it back into focus. Kade nudged her.

Chapter Twenty-One

"What happened?" Jasper demanded.

"Not sure. I think I might have used up a little too much energy." She reached out and tried to contact Kade's mind. Nothing. It had been a waste of effort. She only hoped Flinn had better luck. As if he heard her, he came over to stand beside her.

"Some of Kade's clan will be here in about four hours."

"That's ages away." Amber was exhausted. She couldn't stay awake any longer. She swayed unsteadily.

"Orin and Morgan will stand guard. Get some rest."

Amber frowned, trying to understand Flinn's words. Nothing seemed to make sense anymore.

"My people," Flinn said. "Come on. Before you collapse. You know where Kade's room is."

"She can't sleep in his room," Jasper protested.

"Do either of them look like they're capable of doing anything? And he's stuck as a dragon until those chains come off." Flinn threw his hands up. "Do as you please. I'm not standing around here arguing." He strode towards the house.

Kade nudged Amber and she struggled to walk to the house. Everything seemed so far away. The house looked like it was at the wrong end of binoculars and the ground felt like the swell of the ocean beneath her feet. There was a rushing sound in her ears and everything went dark.

The next thing Amber knew, she was opening her eyes to stare at an off white ceiling, feeling rested. She looked beside her to find Kade curled up on the bed, taking up most of the space. They were in his bed, his forelimbs still chained together. Reaching out with her mind, she checked where everyone was. Crystal was on the opposite side of the house, Flinn near her. Jasper was in the lounge room. Flinn's people were stationed at the front and back doors. She couldn't find anyone else. Amber sat up and Kade immediately opened his eyes and raised his head.

"I'm sorry. Go back to sleep," Amber whispered.

Kade shook his head. He opened his mouth and

a rumble sounded in the back of his throat. His tail flicked once.

Amber reached out her hand to rest it against his scales. "I wish you could speak to me too." She examined the links of the chain, running her fingers over them. The only difference she could see was where they joined the shackle. This time she decided to try fire. Her palm filled with it and she pressed it against the join. Nothing happened. She increased the heat. She glanced worriedly at Kade but his gaze was steady. Then she felt the link give. She pulled against it until it opened. The chain came off the shackle and she went to work on the other side.

Amber dropped the chain onto the floor, her attention on the shackles now. She still couldn't reach Kade's mind so it seemed the shackles were what needed to be removed.

"Interesting."

Amber shrieked when a woman seemed to appear out of thin air. She had bronze hair with streaks of gold and eyes the same colour and shape as Kade's. She was tall, her muscles well developed and Amber wondered if she was what an Amazon warrior would have looked like.

"Kiani?"

"Yes." Kiani picked up the chain from the floor. "Can you do that to the shackles?"

Amber shrugged. "Where did you come from?"

"Oh, I was always here. I was about to let you know when you started playing with fire. I am intrigued. Where did my son find you?"

"He-" Kade growled and Amber turned towards him. He shook his head.

Kiani laughed, a deep sound that filled the room. "I don't blame him. Are there more like you?"

"How do you… disappear? Is there any way to find you when you do? I think Ronan does it."

"Impossible. He isn't Gold. He can't use a Pliethin."

"I couldn't smell him until he had a knife at my throat." Amber's fingers automatically touched where the blade had been. Kade growled. "Then he was suddenly there. I could sense him, smell him. Just like with you."

Kiani frowned. "That is a problem. So he could be outside with his sons."

Amber nodded. She reached out with her mind. Tory and Hound were out the back, where she'd first become a panther, sitting under the trees. She couldn't find Ronan anywhere. "How long can you… stay invisible?"

"Depends on the strength of the ability. I have to

let Bredon know about Ronan." Kiani left the room before Amber could question her further.

The door burst open and Flinn stepped into the room. "There's bloody Gold Dragons popping in and out of the Void all over the house. Deal with them. I didn't expect a dozen of them. Your parents are tolerable. The rest of them aren't."

Crystal followed Flinn into the room, her eyes shining with excitement. "One minute the room is empty, the next there's three or four people staring at you. Then poof, they're gone again."

Flinn's eyes narrowed. "How did the chain come off?"

"I don't recall walking to this room last night," Amber said.

"Your brother carried you here. You passed out mid step," Crystal said.

Amber's stomach rumbled. "I need something to eat."

Crystal paled. "Ah, I wouldn't go into the kitchen right now. There's... ahh... an animal on the table. And lots of blood."

"You better get over your squeamishness in a hurry." Flinn glanced at Crystal before he turned back to Amber. "And I'm still waiting to hear about the chain."

"I burnt them off." Amber ignored Kade's growl. "Can you do anything yet, Crystal?"

Crystal shrugged. "Things keep looking funny to me. I don't know. And I keep hearing sounds that I shouldn't be able to."

"Hawk. You should be able to turn into a hawk. When you figure it out that is." Amber turned to Kade who hissed at the word hawk. "Will you stop? Not being able to understand you is frustrating enough without you constantly trying to get my attention."

"Will I be able to throw fireballs like you?" Crystal came to sit beside her.

Amber took her hand. "I don't know. We can try and see."

"I might as well not be here." Flinn slammed the door shut behind him.

Crystal giggled. "I don't think he's a morning person."

Amber grinned. "I don't think he's a night person either." She glanced at Kade who growled again. "Do you mind?"

Crystal held out her hands. "How do I go about this?"

"I found strong emotion helped."

Crystal snorted. "I'm just about walking on air with

excitement. I can't believe you didn't tell me any of this. I slept in a bed with a dragon! I can hardly believe this is happening."

"Fear, hunger, anger."

"I'm too excited to be afraid. Your brother went into town and got some real food so I've eaten and I've never been able to get as angry as you."

Amber sighed. She took Crystal's hands in hers. Maybe she could draw the power from them like Kade had done for her. She pulled back quickly. "Cold?"

"I felt something. It didn't seem cold." Crystal stared at her hands. She frowned then held her hands out to Amber. "Do that again. I know it's in there, whatever it is."

Amber reluctantly took Crystal's hands. She reached for Crystal's power, pulling at it. She drew her hands back slightly, holding them above Crystal's palms. Fire began to form in her own, Crystal moved her hands down to create more space between them. Ice started to form in Crystal's palms. She squealed excitedly.

Crystal pulled her hands closer to her face to stare at the twin balls of ice glowing in her palms, growing by the second. "I did it. Look, Amber."

Amber stared at their hands thoughtfully. "Hold

that ice. I want to try something." She turned to face Kade who shifted back slightly. "Oh stop being a baby. Brann was willing to let me experiment on him yesterday. Hold out one of your hands… ah… claws… whatever." She pressed the fireball against the shackle, watching as it started to glow with heat. Kade held himself tense, but didn't draw back. She looked over to Crystal. "As soon as I take my hand away, ice this shackle."

Crystal nodded, moving closer. The moment Amber drew back, Crystal forced the ice at the glowing shackle. She shrieked as the shackle exploded into shards and she shielded her face with her hands. Amber threw her arms around Crystal, grinning.

"It worked. I don't know what it's made of, but it worked. It doesn't look or feel like any metal I've ever seen before. I don't even know how normal metal would react to that sort of treatment. But we did it." Amber bounced excitedly on the bed. "Let's do the other one." She turned to Kade. "Oh don't be like that. Hold the shackle out." She ignored his growl.

"I don't think he wants you to remove it like that. Look at the mark we left behind." Crystal pointed to the leathery skin near the claws, which wasn't covered in scales. It was cut in several places and the skin was blistered.

"I'll heal it when we're done." Amber met Kade's gaze. "Come on. We have to get this off you." She pressed a fireball against the shackle as soon as Kade held it out to her. "Now!" She pulled away the moment she thought it was hot enough. She knew what to expect this time, turning her face away as Crystal forced the ice against the metal. She turned back in time to see Kade become human.

"Next time I tell you to get out, you obey." Kade glared at her.

Amber threw her arms around him. "Don't bother giving orders you know I won't follow." She grinned. "We did it. Now let me heal your wrists." It took her a few minutes.

Crystal held out her arm that had been cut by a piece of the shackle. "I don't suppose you can heal humans."

"I don't know. Let me try." Her first attempt failed. It wasn't until she noticed the dragon blood running through Crystal's veins that she had any luck. A wave of exhaustion rushed over her. "Whoops."

"What?" Kade reached out to steady her.

"I think I've got an energy level I can't go past. I might have used it all up."

"Idiot." Kade helped her off the bed. "Let's get you something to eat. That might help."

"Ah, kitchen… dead animal."

Amber touched Crystal's shoulder lightly. "It doesn't bother me."

The door burst open. Flinn stepped into the room and shut the door hard. "How did you do it?" He pointed to Kade.

"We did it." Crystal grinned.

"I didn't give you permission to use my mage." Flinn stood toe to toe with Kade.

Crystal pushed between them, facing Flinn. "I don't need your permission when my best friend asks for my help. And she won't need Kade's permission if I ask her for help. You're going to have to learn to live with that."

"Not everyone who has an issue with following orders will become a renegade, Flinn," Kade said softly. "And you can't stop them from becoming a renegade by controlling their every movement."

"Keep your opinions to yourself." Flinn spun, flung open the door and strode from the room.

Amber turned to Kade. "Do you want to tell me what that was all about?"

"It's none-"

"Don't say it. Crystal has to deal with his moods. Now what was that all about?" Amber's hands went to her hips. Crystal stood beside her, adding her glare.

"His parents became renegades the first year he was in training. They tried to get him to join them. He refused. He hasn't spoken to them since, but a lot of people won't have anything to do with him because of it."

"Why does he resent you so much?"

Kade sighed. "Because I was the only one willing to pair with him for this test."

"You'd think he'd be grateful you did," Crystal said.

Kade shook his head. "You'll soon learn he doesn't like to owe anyone anything."

"So both Flinn and Maira. Anyone else?" Amber asked.

Kade looked uncomfortable. "I think people deserve a chance to prove themselves."

Kiani appeared in the doorway. "It's a major flaw of his. He's too soft. We were beginning to think he'd never make a true Gold Warrior. Then we met you." Her gaze fell on Amber. "Quite a triumph." She turned back to Kade. "Are you going to tell me how you figured that one out?"

Kade shook his head. "Not likely."

Kiani laughed. The same rich laughter of earlier. "I didn't think so. But you have created a difficulty. From the bit I've pieced together from Jasper and

Flinn, Ronan wants his own Dragon Mage and he'll stop at nothing to get one. And the only two in existence are right here in front of me. Anything else you want to add?"

"No. That's about it. Have you found Ronan?"

Kiani shook her head. "And we won't be able to very easily. Have you considered returning to the clan where we can protect you better?"

"Would I fail the test if I did?" Kade shook his head when his mother nodded. "Not an option then. We've only got another seven months to get through."

"I have to go home tonight," Amber said.

"Me too. Angela can only cover for me till six. I'm supposedly with her until then," Crystal said.

"We can provide another six Gold Warriors to help protect you, but that's all we can spare," Kiani said.

Flinn returned to the room. "I need to request a relocation."

"You can only do that under exceptional circumstances. The two of you are meant to be helping each other get through this year. That's the whole idea of pairing everyone." Kiani looked from Flinn to Kade. "I did warn you at the start of the year that personality clashes wouldn't be tolerated."

"My mage doesn't live in this town. I need to be closer to her to protect her," Flinn said.

"Can she move here?" Kiani looked at Crystal, who shook her head.

"I've already tried. I wanted to move with Amber. My parents were adamant this time apart would be good for us. They think we should expand our social circle."

"I'll discuss it with the assessors," Kiani said. "I can't promise anything."

"Ronan wants a mage to help him take back his lands. You can't leave Crystal unprotected. And she has to be home by six. You don't understand how unreasonable our parents can be if we don't follow their rules," Amber said.

"I'll have an answer before then. Information on how to create Dragon Mages would improve your chances of a favourable answer," Kiani said.

"No." Kade and Flinn answered together.

Kiani shrugged. "I can't promise anything."

When Kiani was about to leave the room, Kade reached out to grab her arm. "Remind them what Ronan was like to deal with last time he had a position in our society. He had a lot of followers and powerful friends. I bet they'd back him again. And he always had some plot in progress. With a Dragon Mage, even an untrained one, he'd be unbeatable. And he still eats dragon hearts. It's not like we'd only have to put up with him for a couple of centuries."

Kiani nodded sharply before she left the room.

"Wasn't food mentioned earlier?" Amber asked.

Kade nodded then turned to Flinn. "Did you want something?"

"Your saddle and my mage."

Crystal squealed. "Yes! I'm going flying."

"Take more than your warriors with you," Kade said.

Flinn sneered. "I'm not the idiot around here." He grabbed Crystal's hand, dragging her from the room. Crystal had time for a grin and a wave.

"Now can we eat?" Amber demanded.

Kade's lips slowly curved into a smile. "In a second." He pushed the door shut before he drew Amber close. He stared down at her a moment longer before he lowered his head, his lips meeting hers.

Chapter Twenty-Two

Amber reluctantly stepped outside. Jasper waited for her by his car. Kiani had organised the return of the vehicle and two trailers he'd hired yesterday. Kade walked beside her, an arm around her shoulders. Crystal had already left, being flown back to the city by Flinn, surrounded by three Gold Warriors as well as his two warriors. Before she'd left, Amber and Crystal had removed the chains from Brann and Maira.

She could sense the three warriors that had been assigned to help Kade protect her. Beyond them were Hound and Tory. They'd moved further away, but they were still about. Kade tightened his hold on her as they walked towards Jasper's car.

"I'll follow you home. I'll be within calling distance the entire time. You won't be left unprotected. Not for a second."

"If that was meant to make me feel better, it doesn't."

"It makes me feel better." Kade was solemn for a moment then he grinned. "Your friend said nothing will make you feel better until you've had at least another month to get used to all the changes."

"Great, now you're sharing confidences with Crystal."

"She was sharing confidences with me."

"Oh, that's right. How could I forget? A brick wall shares more information than you do." Amber pulled away from Kade.

He captured her hand, tugging her back to face him. "You and Crystal have been accepted. I can share more information with you now."

"Into your clan?" When Kade nodded, Amber asked, "Both of us?" Another nod. "Is Flinn in your clan too?"

Kade shook his head. "He's clanless. Until we pass all the tests, we're part of the same clan as our parents. His parents are clanless now they're renegades. That's another reason no one wanted to pair with him. If you have only your clan to rely on for help, then it needs to be a strong one."

"Your clan is strong?"

"Yeah."

"Why couldn't they accept him then?"

"Survival of the fittest."

"I hate that comment."

Kade shrugged. "It's the underlying foundation of our entire society. You'll get used to it."

Jasper pushed away from his car. "We're going to be late. And after all the talking I did today, you'll ruin the concessions I won you."

"I'm not grounded?" Amber asked hopefully.

"Dream on. I'm not that good at negotiating. But you're not completely grounded."

Amber threw herself at her brother. "You're the best."

"Yeah well, remember that next time I do something to annoy you." He untangled his sister's arms from him. "Come on. Get in the car and let's go and deal with all the dramas."

Amber turned back to Kade. She smiled slightly. "I'll see you later." He nodded before he became a dragon and took to the sky.

Jasper shook his head. "Every time I see that, it completely throws me. How the hell did you manage to keep it to yourself? At least I can talk to you and Crystal about it."

"It just about killed me." She hopped in the car. "Not that anyone would have believed me. I think they would've thought I was on drugs or had lost the plot."

Jasper nodded as he started the car. "Tell me about it. I wonder how many other humans know dragons exist."

Amber shrugged. "Who knows?"

"And they're not what I would've thought they'd be like. You know, the two opposites they're mostly portrayed as. Protectors or devourers of virgins."

"They're sort of like us. They have their own laws, they have good and bad people and most of them are only looking out for themselves. The only difference is their survival of the fittest belief. That's the one thing I can't stomach."

"When you think about it, we believed that centuries ago. Maybe they need to believe that for genetic reasons. I got the impression they don't have many offspring. Maybe only the strongest can reproduce."

Amber shrugged. "What did you tell Mum and Grandma?"

Jasper grinned. "I'm a genius."

"And did they laugh when you told them that?"

Jasper chuckled. "It's a fact. I am. Grandma is the most mercenary person imaginable. She probably still has the first cent she ever earned under lock and key.

I told her Kade's parents were independently wealthy and spent their time flying to different countries."

Amber laughed. "Flying!" She couldn't stop grinning at that thought. "And they swallowed that?"

"Well, I asked Kiani if she could do a rich snob act and visit them on her way home today."

"Did she?"

"She was brilliant. She even turned up in a limo. Can you imagine that? She told them she didn't want attention drawn to the fact her family were attending school here as she thought they deserved time away from the limelight that excessive wealth creates. And she was covered by a fortune in jewels. You could see Grandma's mouth watering while she estimated the total cost of them. Mum was sceptical. But it wasn't like she could argue Kiani's presence. Even I wouldn't normally be able to pull together such an elaborate hoax."

"And what about me being grounded?"

"Kiani really laid it on thick about her poor motherless niece and how you were the first friend she'd made since she'd lost her parents. She had Mum feeling guilty about setting Maira's emotional growth back with her interference. She was absolutely brilliant." Jasper grinned. "She's my new idol. I want to be able to manipulate people like she can."

"You're evil!"

"Yep."

"How did she explain all the others living with Kade and Maira?"

"The offspring of long-term family retainers. Seriously, I don't know how Mum managed to grill her as much as she did. She was highly snobbish, utterly unapproachable and absolutely brilliantly manipulative."

"She's already married," Amber said dryly. "And about a century old."

"She looks good for a woman that old." Jasper grinned then sobered. "You do realise you and Crystal are going to outlive the rest of us, don't you?"

Amber nodded. "I know a lot of people would be thrilled by that idea. It scares me. Kade said I won't age as fast. How am I going to explain to Mum and Dad why I'm still looking so young a decade from now?"

"Plastic surgery?"

"You're a great help." She hit her brother's arm with the back of her hand.

"It's possible."

"And I'll have the money needed to afford that? Yeah right!"

"Your new best friend Maira can pay for it. Oh,

and while I remember, your relationship with Kade is platonic. I don't think Mum could handle thoughts of you sharing a bed with Kade, even if he was in dragon form."

"And what if she catches us together in a less than platonic situation?"

Jasper shrugged. "Relationships change. Stop looking for problems. Haven't you got enough to deal with?"

"More than enough." She momentarily rested her hand on her brother's forearm. "I wish you weren't going home tonight."

"You'll be fine."

"But you deal with Mum so much better than I do."

"I need some sort of ability. It's not like I can throw fireballs at people who piss me off."

Amber laughed. "You'd better remember that next time you decide to annoy me." Her smile disappeared as they pulled up in front of Helen's house. "Time for battle."

"See, that's where you go wrong. How about time for negotiations?"

"Maybe."

"Oh, and Amber?"

"Yeah?"

Jasper stared at her for a moment. "If you ever

come across another dragon looking for a mage, remember you've got a brother."

Amber nodded, her expression solemn. "I'll remember, but I also won't hold you to it if you figure out it's not as good as you think it is."

"Fair enough. Just as long as you let me know."

"I promise."

Helen and Donna waited in the kitchen for them. Amber sat quietly in the seat her mother pointed to. She was relieved when her brother also took a seat. Silence filled the room. Amber looked at her hands clasped on the table. There wasn't much she could say without getting herself into more trouble. It was always better to wait and see which tactic her mother would use.

"You never told me Maira and Kade are wealthy."

Amber shrugged. "It didn't seem important."

"Their parents don't have to work a single day in their lives and you don't think that's important to mention. People like that don't even think the same way we do," Donna said.

"They do so."

"Don't argue with your mother," Helen snapped.

Amber opened her mouth to argue with Helen instead.

Jasper spoke first. "They don't act rich. Well, the

kids don't. Kade's parents are a little over the top. Kade and Maira want to live a normal life for a bit and see what it's like."

"They have different values to us," Donna said.

"They think nothing of wearing all that flashy gear around and lording it over the rest of us," Helen said.

"Does that mean I can't hang out with them anymore?"

"Don't be stupid. Get the boy to marry you and you'll never have to work a day in your life," Helen said.

"Mother." Donna dragged the word out.

Helen shrugged. "He seems nice enough. She'll be eighteen in a bit over a year. They'd probably be divorced by the time she's twenty, but at least she'd be able to go him for a nice chunk of change."

Amber shook her head. She shouldn't have been surprised. When did her grandmother ever act like a sweet, little old lady? "I'm not interested in getting married. Even to make a fortune by divorcing. Come on Grandma, that's plain mean."

"Your loss." Helen shrugged.

Amber turned to her mother. "You haven't told me if I can still see Maira."

"Yes, but only because her aunt said she was finding it difficult to get past the death of her parents.

She's never looked like a child grieving the couple of times I've met her. Weekdays she's welcome to visit you here. Weekends you can go out one day together. That's it. The rest of the time I expect you to be at home."

"Mum!"

"Don't start, Amber. You're lucky to be going anywhere after the stunt you pulled this weekend."

"I wouldn't be letting her go anywhere," Helen said. "Unless she was going after that boy."

Amber clenched her teeth, trying to hold back her anger. Her panther struggled to break free. She almost became a panther when she was surprised by a hawk that also tried to escape. She grinned. It had worked.

"What's so funny?" Donna demanded.

She met Jasper's gaze, looking for inspiration. He shrugged slightly. Her gaze fell on her grandmother before she turned back to her mother. "I've got Grandma trying to sell me off to the highest bidder and for most of my life you've pretty much encouraged me to keep my legs crossed and no dating until I've finished uni."

"I don't find it the least bit amusing." Donna turned to her mother. "And you can stop trying to matchmake. I don't care if he's rich enough to own his own country."

Amber giggled. Did 'lands' count as owning your own country? She shook her head when her mother looked at her again. "Can I go to my room now? I've got homework to do."

"Dinner in an hour." Donna reached out to pat Jasper's hand. "Are you staying for dinner?"

He shook his head. "I want to get on the road before it gets too busy. Will you walk me to my car, Amber?"

Amber rose to her feet, waiting for Jasper to finish receiving hugs and kisses. They walked silently to the car. "Thanks for that."

"You've got to learn not to bite back. Grandma was a bit of a laugh though. I wonder if she says anything to Kade."

Amber laughed at the thought of Helen trying to set up a date for her. "God, I hope not. She's such a pain."

"You'll survive her."

"I just want to come home. I bet Kade would be able to move if I did. Flinn was given permission."

"I don't think Dad would have been as lenient. Part of it was that Mum had Grandma drooling over all their money and completely changing her view about them."

"I still want to go home," Amber said stubbornly.

"Take care, little sister. Try not to let Ronan close enough to grab you." Jasper hugged her lightly.

"You take care too. Oh no!" Amber's eyes widened. She reached out to find Kade. *"You have to send one of the warriors to watch over Jay. If Ronan caught him I'd work for him."*

"That reduces the amount to protect you."

"What's wrong?" Jasper asked.

"You could surround me with a dozen warriors, but if my family were in his hands, it wouldn't matter. It'd be the same as if he caught me."

"Amber?" Jasper tried to get her attention again.

"Done. Tell Jay that Shannon will watch over him. She's a Gold Warrior who's passed her second test. Sorry. None of the others were willing to change orders at first."

"You've got your own dragon to guard you now," Amber told her brother.

"What do I need that for?"

"Because I wouldn't leave you in Ronan's hands if he caught you. Her name's Shannon."

"That won't leave you short?"

Amber grinned. "I'll be fine. Now don't go

thinking you're being stalked by a female because of your looks. She's only guarding you for me."

Jasper laughed. "I'll try not to let it go to my head." He opened the car door and glanced back one last time before he got in and drove off.

Amber sensed a dragon flying above her brother's car. Relieved, she went inside. Only her mother was in the kitchen now. Amber hurried through the kitchen before Donna could think of anything else to say to her. Kade was lying on her bed when she entered her room and locked the door behind her.

Chapter Twenty-Three

"You're going to get caught in here one day." Amber stood by the bed.

Kade grinned. "Your grandmother would probably march me to a priest and have us married off and divorced quicker than you could change into a panther."

"Stop listening into conversations you weren't invited to."

"Then I wouldn't hear anything interesting." Kade rolled off the bed, landing in front of her. "So I take it your grandmother's proposal doesn't suit?"

"Stop joking about it. I'm only sixteen."

Kade laughed. "Not nearly seventeen?"

"Oh shut up. And what did you mean about none of the warriors were willing to change orders at first?"

"Shannon said she'd watch Jay if I considered her for my third test. Suddenly the others were offering their help in exchange for me taking them on for whatever test they were required to do next."

"How many tests are there?"

"Ten."

"Do you have to do them in order?"

Kade shook his head. "Usually easiest to. The higher the test, the harder it is and the more Gold Warriors are allowed to work together on it. Most Golds aren't willing to join someone who has only recently passed one test." Kade grinned. "Having my own mage suddenly makes me a desirable partner."

"What's the next test?"

"Cleaning out a wyvern nest."

"Is that hard?"

"Probably similar to a hunter going bare handed to take care of a pride of lions."

"You've got to be kidding. And they expect you to do that for your third test? What's the hardest one?"

"Taking your own lands and holding them for a year."

"How long does it take to get through the ten tests?"

"Some people never make it through them."

"What about those that are clanless?" She couldn't help thinking about Flinn.

"They can always become a warrior for someone else."

Amber couldn't see Flinn willing to give up his Gold status to become one of the 'dispensable warriors'. He'd rather die first. If she'd known all this, she would never have linked Crystal's future with his. "Flinn… Crystal… I–"

"Stop panicking. I know Flinn would never choose that option. As long as he wants, he has a place at my side. I can't force him to keep working with me, but I won't turn him away."

"Why? And don't give me any crap about everyone deserving a chance."

Kade sighed, turning away from her. "His father saved me from wyverns when I was barely a decade old. He didn't need to. He would've been within the laws to leave me to try and survive on my own abilities. He isn't… wasn't even from our clan. Then when I offered to pair with Flinn since no one else would, his father came to see me. He said his favour for saving me was that I'd always stand by his son in the tests for as long as he was willing to accept me at his side. Maybe I wouldn't have been willing after putting up with him this time. I don't know. I swore I would. So I will. Dragons must honour their word. It's the law."

Amber rested her hand against Kade's back. His skin was warm beneath her palm. "You would. No one's making you keep Maira and I know she annoys the hell out of you at times."

"She's loyal. I can put up with a few disagreements for loyalty."

Amber moved so she could meet Kade's gaze. She grinned. "So's Flinn… to himself."

Kade laughed. "I can't argue with that." He pulled her close, inhaling the scent of her skin. "The hawk you told me of earlier, have you tried turning into it yet?"

"No. The panther keeps ahead of it. I'm beginning to wonder if I should have done that. But I was worried about splattering on the ground if I ever fell off you."

"Then I guess it's time to practice becoming a hawk."

"I've got homework to do."

"Maira can do it for you."

Amber shook her head. "And how am I meant to pass my exams if I don't learn the work?"

"They aren't important. You're a Dragon Mage."

"What has that got to do with anything?"

"You'll always have a place at my side."

Amber shook her head. "No. I want to do more with my life than be your mage."

"Amber–"

"Not interested. I hate your survival of the fittest belief. I won't live by it. I'll help you if I think I can, but I'm not going to spend my life being only your mage. I want a life too."

"Fine. We'll do your homework first. Then you practice becoming a hawk."

Amber smiled sweetly. "Don't worry. You'll eventually learn it's easiest to give in at the start of the argument."

Kade growled in answer.

* * *

Amber grinned when she logged into her messenger and saw Crystal had changed her name. She glanced up as Kade came in the French doors and made his way to her bed, a smile for her in greeting. He flopped onto the bed, picking up his schoolbooks she'd brought home for him. Amber turned back to her laptop.

Amber says: I take it you've mastered the change?

Hawkgirl says: It's amazing. Flinn thinks I should be able to do it quicker. Told me fifteen seconds is too long. What does he want? One second?

Amber says: lol. Probably. But you'll get better.

Hawkgirl says: I hope so. You are truly my very best friend. If you never give me another birthday or Xmas pressie I won't complain.

Amber says: I'm taking a print screen, in case you forget you said that.

Hawkgirl says: Ha ha. Wish you could stay here this weekend. I can't believe it's Friday again!!

Amber says: Tell me about it! The days are flying.

Hawkgirl says: In more than the usual sense :)

Amber says: lol. You seen Jay?

Hawkgirl says: Yeah. You should see his babysitter!!!! If I was into girls I'd be chasing after her. She's not what you'd call inconspicuous. And yet at times she appears from nowhere.

Amber says: It might be one of her abilities.

Hawkgirl says: Yeah well, wish I had that one.

Amber says: Figured out any more?

Hawkgirl says: Nah. Ice and hawk. But I'm not complaining. Flinn doesn't like the ice. He said Golds and ice don't mix. Well, isn't that a good thing?

Amber says: You'd think.

Hawkgirl says: I pointed out that he can't breathe fire yet so it doesn't matter.

Amber says: Bet that went down well.

Hawkgirl says: Yeah, he can't take criticism.

Amber says: rofl.

Hawkgirl says: He certainly wasn't ;)

Amber says: Wish you could come here since I can't go there.

Hawkgirl says: Parents! Mine said I can't go see you till next term because you're grounded. Way to go!? Punish me too : (almost enough to make you run away from home ;)

Amber says: Ha ha. Comedian!

Hawkgirl says: Ohh…. That's right, you tried that. Big fail!

Amber says: Gee thanks… not!

Hawkgirl says: I'd better go. Have to set up the weekend with Inge. I feel kind of bad that Flinn has Orin keeping her entertained while the rest of us train. But at least she's not stuck with Flinn. He'd make a good boot camp instructor!!!

Amber says: That doesn't surprise me. But Inge is cool about it. She said she knows he's only with her to give you and Flinn time together. She thinks it's sweet Flinn and Orin are such good friends. And she said he's fun to be with.

Hawkgirl says: I know she keeps saying that, but well, I still wonder if she really means it.

Amber says: Does she strike you as the type to suffer in silence?

Hawkgirl says: lol. No!

Amber says: Then stop worrying.

Hawkgirl says: K. Will do. Bibi.

Amber says: Later.

Amber quickly replied to an email from Angela, glanced through her other messages then exited everything before pulling up a document to start her assignment.

"How long will you be on your laptop?"

Amber leaned back in her seat to look at Kade. "I don't know. Couple of hours?"

"I've never done so much homework as I've done since I started spending my afternoons with you."

"It'll do you good. I've had nearly twelve years of it. And you're complaining about one year."

Kade shrugged. "It's impractical. There's no point to it."

"Yes there is."

"What?"

"To keep as many teenagers off the street as possible." Amber grinned when Kade rolled his eyes.

"Don't worry, it'll be school holidays in about three weeks and then you'll have two weeks without homework. Although we'll probably have a few assignments to do."

Kade sat up. His lips slowly curved into a smile.

"Stop thinking. Whatever you're planning it doesn't look good."

His smile became a grin. "I've requested the list of wyvern nests that need cleaning out."

"No."

Kade rose to his feet. "We can get it done in a few days. There's nothing that says we can't have mages help us. The only limits set are three Gold Dragons and two warriors per Gold. Apart from that, we can use whatever we think might aid us."

"So you could have other dragons help you as long as they weren't warriors?"

"Yeah, but they wouldn't be any help. If they haven't been trained how to fight, a wyvern would slaughter them. What do you say?"

"Have you talked to Flinn?"

Kade shook his head. "As if he'd disagree. He needs to do the tests as soon as possible. And Shannon has been complaining her warriors have been sitting around getting fat while she's been looking out for your brother."

Amber's mobile phone rang. She drew it from her pocket, glancing at the display. The number was private. "Hello?"

"Hello, mage."

"Ronan?" She brushed Kade's hand away when he tried to take the phone from her.

"I've got more time than you have. You might as well give in now. They're not going to protect you forever."

She refused to give in to the fear his words caused. "You haven't done too well so far."

"Amber!" Kade glared at her. "Stop goading him."

Ronan laughed. "Is it stupidity or spirit?"

"I prefer to think spirit."

"Maybe I should have had a human child. That's the one thing my sons are lacking."

"You never had daughters?"

"I left them with their mothers."

"That might have been your second mistake."

"What was my first?"

"Demanding complete obedience so your sons had no chance to develop any spirit." She pushed Kade away again and moved over to the French doors to put some space between them. He followed, even when she frowned at him.

"You owe me a Pliethin."

Amber smiled at the abrupt change in topic. "And a few grand as well."

"The money is unimportant. I have more than I'll ever be able to spend. The Pliethin is what I'll miss the most."

"You aren't a Gold Dragon. It wasn't any use to you." Amber kept moving knowing it would make it harder for Kade to hear Ronan's side of the conversation.

"But it was mine. I caught it. I put it in the box. And while I had it, that was one less Gold Dragon that could use it."

"Sorry. I gave it to a Gold Warrior. It seemed wasteful leaving it shut up in a box." She slapped Kade's hand as he tried to take the phone again.

"Meet with me."

"We've already come to the conclusion that I'm not stupid."

"We discussed it. No conclusion was reached."

"I'm not going to meet with you. You're wasting your time."

"My time to waste. And I certainly have a lot of it."

"You haven't got anything I want. I'm not interested in helping you get your lands back and I certainly don't want you to have any power in dragon society. I don't like your methods of getting things done." She couldn't help wondering what sort of dragon would eat the heart of one of their sons.

"Why'd you take the Pliethin?"

"Because I knew someone who could use it."

"A clanless Gold Warrior who can't help you in any way."

"I'm not a dragon. I don't think like dragons."

"It's strange how that same clanless dragon now has his own mage."

"Life is full of oddities."

"Even stranger that she's a close friend of yours."

"Might be something in the water."

"I think it's something to do with the Pliethin."

"You're welcome to think what you want."

"I captured another Pliethin today."

Amber struggled to think of an answer. "Should I pop open a bottle of champagne?"

Ronan laughed. "That hesitation was rather telling."

"No hesitation. Kade keeps trying to take the phone off me. He doesn't believe I should be talking to you."

"I'm willing to make someone a Dragon Mage. The terms are one year service to me. One year from any year during the next five. I can be flexible. Then they can go their own way. I have the Pliethin I believe is needed to make the change."

Jasper came instantly to mind. Why had he asked her that? Great! Now she was going to have to let him know about the offer. She hoped he wouldn't want to accept Ronan's proposition. He was a cannibal.

"Do I take it you have someone in mind?"

"Text me your number. I'll get back to you next week. I'm not promising anything. And call your sons home."

"This isn't a ploy to take off is it?"

Amber laughed sharply. "How well do you know the human world? I'm still living with my parents and going to school. I'm a little tied to this spot of the world at the moment." She'd considered running, but had worried that would put her family in danger.

"One week truce. Then I'll expect you to contact me."

"I will." When Ronan hung up, Amber stared at her phone, wondering how he'd got her number. A text came through in less than a minute. It was Ronan's number. She looked over to Kade who watched her carefully. How was she going to explain everything to him when he looked like he wanted to hunt Ronan down?

"What have you agreed to?"

"Nothing exactly."

"Then why do you look like you're about to tell me you gave away my lands?"

Amber was unable to meet his gaze. "Can you find out exactly why Ronan lost his lands and who has them now? And would it be a really bad idea if he got them back and what are the chances of him getting them in the space of a year?"

"What did you promise?"

"Nothing." She was finally able to bring herself to meet his gaze. "Yet."

"Amber-"

When she heard the warning in his voice she hurriedly filled him in on the parts of the conversation he'd missed. He remained silent. "Are you going to say anything?"

Kade turned away from her as he shook his head.

"Kade-"

"Quiet for a minute."

She waited impatiently. Finally, he turned back to face her. "Well?"

"I should have the information you requested within a couple of days. I've asked Maira to contact some people. And if it turns out the people who have his lands are the original owners?"

Amber shrugged. "I don't know. It'll be up to Jay."

"Will he care one way or the other?"

Amber didn't hesitate. "Yes."

"I hope so."

Chapter Twenty-Four

Amber reached out to Shannon to let her know she was nearly there. She saw Jasper's window was open, the screen removed. Pulling in her wings, she soared through the gap to land on the floor. Her change to human wasn't very graceful and she stumbled, barely catching her balance. But she was getting better. At least she no longer landed on her face. She reached out with her mind and checked that Kade and his warriors were on the roof, like they'd said they would be, so she could talk to her brother alone. There was only three days until she had to meet with Ronan. Her stomach lurched. She didn't like either of their options.

Jasper stood beside Shannon and grinned at her. "Neat trick."

Amber's answering smile was forced. "Glad to entertain you."

"What's up?"

Amber gestured towards the bed. When they were sitting side by side, she cleared her throat. Where to begin? "You know the dragon who's trying to get me to help him?"

"The one who kidnapped you?"

"Yeah." She glanced over to Shannon, wondering how to ask her to leave without offending her.

"Call me when you want me to return." Shannon jumped out the window.

"You didn't have to chase her off," Jasper complained.

"It's probably best I did. We found out some information about him."

"And? I do want to get to bed sometime before midnight."

Amber rose to her feet, unable to sit still. "It's your fault you know."

"How can him kidnapping you be my fault?" Jasper got to his feet, a frown wrinkling his brow.

"No. You wanted to know if a dragon wanted a mage. He does and he has the means to make you one. Well, half the means. He asks for a year service in return. And he's no worse than the ones who currently hold his lands and they were his originally."

"You're not explaining yourself very well."

"Probably not. Okay, here's the deal. Ronan, who at first glance looks like the bad guy, is actually the victim. Well, regarding the theft of his lands anyway. He's even a little less unpleasant than the dragon who currently holds his lands. And that was a surprise. The only difference is that the one holding them now doesn't have as much influence in their society as Ronan did." Amber paused. Now came the part she really didn't want to tell her brother. "Ronan has half the ingredients needed to make you a Dragon Mage. The price is a year's service to him while trying to get his lands back. But I've got a feeling he may extend that year if you fail and try to claim you didn't give your full effort to the endeavour. You'll probably have to pledge service to another dragon for the other ingredient needed. A Gold Dragon. We don't know if you can make two mages using the same Gold. So it'd probably be best to find another one instead."

"Like Shannon?"

"Yeah."

"What does Kade think?"

"He's biased."

"What did he say?"

Amber hesitated. "It'll stop Ronan from trying to kidnap me and he'll have another mage he can entice the services of a Gold Warrior with."

Jasper laughed. "Nice to see he's at least willing to protect you."

"Yeah well, we had a big fight about it."

"You shouldn't have. I was thinking the same thing. Well, about Ronan anyway. How long have I got to decide?"

"Three days. I have to ring him Friday."

"Where's Kade?"

She checked again. "On the roof."

"Call him in. I want to talk to him. Without you here. And there's no point in glaring at me like that. It won't change my mind."

"Fine." Amber changed into a hawk and flew out the window. She reached out to Kade with her mind. *"He wants to see you. Probably wants to do the stupid big brother protector thing."* She could feel Kade's amusement.

"Don't go far. Stick with Maira and Brann."

Amber joined them on the roof, changing into human form before she sat beside them.

"Have you been kicked out too?" Maira grinned. "Males often think only they can plan things."

"I bet Jay's grilling Kade about how long we can keep Ronan from kidnapping me."

Maira's grin became a wistful smile. "That must be

nice. Having a blood brother who cares enough to put himself in danger to protect you."

"I'd do the same for him."

"My family isn't like that. They take survival of the fittest to the extreme."

They sat together in silence until Kade flew up to the roof, landing beside them. As soon as he was human, he reached out for Amber's hand. "Jay has conditions of his own. Organise a meeting for Friday night. Tell Ronan we're opening negotiations. We're not expecting to finalise anything then."

"Are you certain Jay will be safe helping Ronan?"

"If he decides to go ahead, we'll all help him."

"Even Flinn?"

Kade laughed. "Not all of the tests are spelled out clearly. Some of them consist of taking on jobs for warriors that are of sufficient difficulty to prove our abilities. Taking lands back for someone is considered to be one of the most difficult tasks. Getting another test completed is always a priority for Flinn."

"I didn't know. I wish you wouldn't be so stingy with your information."

"We discussed the possibility of attacking over the Christmas break. He should have enough time off from uni to be able to manage if we have all the planning in place beforehand. But, we both think starting out with an easier battle first would be a good idea."

"Your wyvern test," Amber said dryly.

Kade nodded. "It makes sense."

"I'm sure it does. What are his other conditions?"

"That Ronan isn't there to see the process. And he's to stop consuming the hearts of his enemies and if his lands are regained with less than a year of service, the year is considered complete. And Ronan is to never attack, harm, blackmail or restrain any of us again or help anyone else to do any of those things."

"What are the chances he'll go for it?"

Kade shrugged. "We'll have to wait and see. He's always been unpredictable."

"The only thing that bugs me about all this," Maira said, "is we're going to help him after he had us chained and locked up."

Brann pulled Maira close. "Get used to it. How often do clans change loyalty in the space of a century? The people we're attacking today could be our best friends tomorrow. You should know half of it is politics."

"It still bugs me," Maira muttered.

"Me too," Amber said.

"Do you want to go and talk to your brother again before we go home?" Kade asked.

Amber nodded. "Yeah. I have to tell him he's an idiot." She grinned.

Maira laughed. "Good. Tell him I think he is too. Practical, but still an idiot."

"Okay." Amber rose to her feet and changed into a hawk. For some reason it was harder to change when she was sitting.

Chapter Twenty-Five

They were seated around Kade's kitchen table. Ronan, Kade, Amber, Flinn, Jasper and Crystal. Everyone else, including Ronan's two sons, were in the lounge room. So far there'd only been silence from in there.

"Are you sure you don't want me chained and left in a dungeon for the rest of my life too?" Ronan glanced around the table.

"I considered it, but for some reason I didn't think you'd agree to it." Amber grinned at him.

Ronan chuckled. "I'm sure you did." His expression became thoughtful as he turned to Jasper. "Putting you in the service of a young Gold makes sense. Some training is always a benefit. And I would have your word that you would all participate in capturing my lands?"

"You would have to list your request with the Elders so we can claim it for a test," Kade said.

"You don't expect we're doing it out of love do you?" Flinn glared at Ronan.

Ronan shook his head. "End of the year will give me time to do all the planning. Hopefully it'll give Jasper time to learn his abilities, although some of them can take years to make themselves known."

"And you're to share all the information you gather, regardless of how important or unimportant you think it is," Kade said.

"Only regarding the capture of my lands." Ronan turned his gaze on Amber. "You and yours are only safe from me for as long as you live. You get yourself killed and everyone is fair game again. And you cannot claim everyone you meet as yours. It isn't limitless." When Amber nodded, Ronan looked towards Kade. "I have one final condition. That I will be allowed to one more time consume one entire dragon heart. Either enemy or renegade. Beaten in battle by one of my people or myself."

Kade's fingers drummed on the table as he met Ronan's gaze. He didn't look away even with the conversation in his head between nearly all the others seated at the table. Only Jasper and Ronan were excluded.

"I can't see him completely giving in on that subject," Flinn said.

"How will that help him?" Amber asked.

"He can leave it at least another five hundred years before he has it, maybe even a century. He will age, but not like a human does. That'll give him another one to two centuries in total," Kade said.

Amber managed to hold back her grin. *"Two centuries. The amount of time before he planned to retire anyway."*

"Take the offer and be done with it. We get another mage and we'll learn how to take lands from the best. It should make our final test easier," Flinn said.

Kade's fingers stilled. "We accept."

Ronan rose to his feet. "The Pliethin will be delivered tonight. I'll send regular intelligence updates as I receive them."

Everyone else rose from the table, unwilling to be seated while Ronan stood. Kade held out his hand, which Ronan took. "I'll see you towards the end of the year."

Ronan turned to Amber. "See me out."

"Amber-" Kade turned to her.

She pushed him from her mind. Even though it had sounded more like an order than a request, Amber treated it like a request and nodded in agreement. She fell in beside Ronan as he headed out the back door. She sensed the dragons in the lounge room move to the front of the house. When they were far enough from the house, she stopped to face him, meeting his intense look. She remained silent, waiting for him to speak first, grateful for the practice she'd received when her father used the same tactic.

Ronan grinned. "No demands as to what I want?"

Amber shrugged. "I guess you'll tell me when you finish playing your little game."

He laughed. "I'm going to enjoy working with you. I don't know why I didn't take a closer look at humans centuries ago. But you always seemed such frail creatures with ridiculously short life spans that it never seemed worth the effort. And Dragon Mages were raised amongst their dragon clans. This is a more interesting way of doing things."

"I hope you won't be offended that I'm not looking forward to working with you."

"Not at all. I've always enjoyed a challenge. We'll be friends before my lands are captured."

"You've got to be kidding me." Amber stared at him in surprise. That was the last thing she'd expected him to say. "Friends?"

"Of a fashion. At least not enemies, anyway." He smiled, a predatory one that made Amber worry even more. "I've figured out you don't know anything about being a mage. I'm willing to teach you. Think about it before you dismiss the idea."

"Why?"

"Because it'll benefit me."

"Then why not Crystal or Jay?"

"Because I like you. And you're capable of passing the knowledge along. Besides, Flinn wouldn't let me near Crystal on my own and Jasper doesn't trust me in the slightest."

"I don't trust you either."

"Actually, I think you do. You're standing here with me, aren't you?"

Amber frowned. "Okay, maybe I trust you to stick to the agreement because you always keep your word. But that's it. I don't really trust you."

"That's enough. You have my number if you want to learn." Ronan became a dragon and took to the sky.

Amber stood there, watching as he disappeared. She felt Kade's presence before he reached her side, leaning against him as he draped his arm around her.

"What did he want?"

Amber recounted their conversation. "I keep thinking I should take him up on his offer at the same time as I'm telling myself I'm insane."

Kade smiled. "You are insane. Do you know how many people, both dragon and human, Ronan has killed because they've annoyed him? Not angered, just annoyed."

"Maybe you better not tell me."

Kade sighed. He faced her, his hands resting on her hips. "I must be insane too. I think you should learn from him. No one else has the knowledge he has. I'd be within calling distance. Not hovering like Flinn would. You'd have the space you need to learn. Besides, he'll keep his word not to harm you. He never breaks his word."

She stared up at him for a moment before she wrapped her arms around him, pressing her lips to his. She allowed sensation to temporarily take over before she reluctantly pulled back. "The future terrifies me, but I'm glad you landed on my balcony."

"Me too." Kade stared down at her for a second before he grinned. "Does that mean you're looking forward to wyvern hunting in a few weeks?"

Amber groaned theatrically. "Don't remind me about it. You've still got to convince my mum to let me go for the entire holidays." She smiled slyly. "You mightn't be able to manage it."

Kade shook his head. "Your brother says he has that all under control."

"Huh. He would. I can't believe how bloodthirsty he is about the wyverns." Another thought occurred to her. "Where will we stay?"

"On clan lands."

Amber grinned. "Yes! I can't wait." She was sure to be able to find out more information about dragons, and Kade's clan in particular, by staying on his lands.

"Neither can I." Kade's lips met hers again. "Two weeks where I won't have to pretend things are platonic between us."

Amber felt a thrill go through her as she thought of what that meant. Two weeks. She couldn't get the words to stop repeating in her mind. "Being away for two weeks won't interfere with your current test?"

"No. People go away during school holidays. It fits in with what your society expects."

Crystal called out from the back door. "Are you two going to spend all day out there? At least get a bed instead of being exhibitionists. Otherwise, we're waiting on you to start our war council."

"Bed or war council?" Kade asked Amber.

She laughed.

He shook his head, amusement filling his eyes. "Maybe I better not let you make that decision. If you said bed I'd be left wondering if it was only to get out of making battle plans. Come on, time for a war council."

Amber linked her fingers through Kade's, walking back to the house at his side. She glanced around. Maybe it wouldn't be so bad staying around here after all. And it wasn't even for a full year. As soon as school finished for the year she was headed back to Brisbane. Her mum wouldn't be able to stop her. She could manage sticking around that long. She looked up at Kade as she felt the panther and hawk stir in her. Well, she could manage that now. Although she was still uncertain about how to deal with Ronan. But she better figure it out fast because she was absolutely certain he believed in survival of the fittest.

Free Ebook

Subscribe to Avril's newsletter and receive a free ebook. This ebook is exclusive to those on her mailing list. To find out more about this offer visit:

www.avrilsabine.com/free-ebook

*

We value your privacy and will not sell, rent, exchange or loan your email address to third parties. Your information is confidential and you are under no obligation to remain on the mailing list and can unsubscribe at any time.

Acknowledgements

Thank you to everyone who helped make this series better.

To The Reader

If you enjoyed this book, why not consider leaving a review to help other readers discover it too? Reader engagement is one of the few ways that lets an author know readers want more books in a particular series or genre. So leave a review and tell friends, not only about this book but also about other ones you've enjoyed, so you can continue to enjoy books by your favourite authors for years to come.

Dreams are meant to be lived,

Avril.

About The Author

Avril is an Australian author who lives with her family on acreage in South East Queensland. She writes mostly young adult and children's speculative fiction, but has been known to dabble in other genres. You can find more information about her at www.avrilsabine.com where you can also subscribe to her newsletter to be kept informed about new releases, current projects, blog posts and exclusive news.

Titles By Avril Sabine

Stories about strong characters and characters who discover their strengths.

SERIES

Assassins Of The Dead- Young Adult Fantasy/ Paranormal

Book 1: Dark Blade

Book 2: Dragon Touched

Book 3: Society Against Vampires

Book 4: King's Request

Dragon Blood- Young Adult Urban Fantasy (with elements of romance)

(5 book series)

Book 1: Pliethin

Book 2: Wyvern

Book 3: Surety

Book 4: Knight

Book 5: Mage

Dragon Mage- Young Adult Urban Fantasy (with elements of romance)

(Series two of Dragon Blood series)

Book 1: Promise

Dragon Blood Chronicles- Young Adult Urban Fantasy (with elements of romance)

(Companion stand alone series to Dragon Blood)

Book 1: Oath

Book 2: Betrayed

Guardians Of The Round Table- Young Adult Fantasy LitRPG

(Co-written with Storm and Rhys Petersen)

Book 1: Dexterity Fail

Book 2: Goblin Boots

Book 3: Singed Feathers

Book 4: Frog Mage

Book 5: Crystal Mine

Book 6: Cursed Harp

Rosie's Rangers- Young Adult Western Steampunk

(6 book series)

Book 1: Justice

Book 2: Vengeance

Book 3: Treachery

Book 4: Accused

Book 5: Wanted

Book 6: Corruption

Mark Of Kings- Children's Fantasy

(Upper middle grade/preteen)

(4 book series)

Book 1: The Arena

Book 2: The Island

Book 3: The Assassin

Book 4: The King

STAND ALONE SERIES

Demon Hunters- Young Adult Urban Fantasy/ Horror (with elements of romance)

Book 1: Blood Sacrifice

Book 2: Retribution

Book 3: Tainted

Book 4: Premonition

Book 5: Cursed

Book 6: Feud

Book 7: Extrication

Plea Of The Damned- *Young Adult Urban Fantasy/Paranormal*

(6 book series)

Book 1: Forgive Me Lucy

Book 2: Forgive Me Aiden

Book 3: Forgive Me Jena

Book 4: Forgive Me Kobe

Book 5: Forgive Me Marti

Book 6: Forgive Me Dawson

**Realms Of The Fae- *Young Adult Urban Fantasy*
*(with elements of romance)***

The Sword (short story in Like A Girl Anthology)

Heart Of Stone

Book 1: A Debt Owed

Book 2: Marked By The Hunt

Book 3: The Magic Collector

Book 4: An Unexpected Betrayal

Book 5: Imprisoned By Iron

Fairytales Retold (Short Stories)

Snow-White And Rose-Red

The Twelve Brothers

The Light Princess

Beauty And The Beast

Sleeping Beauty

Aschenputtel

The Golden Bird

The Frog Prince

The Death Of Koshchei The Deathless

Myths And Legends Retold (Short Stories)

Ion, Son Of Apollo

Sir Gawain And The Maid With The Narrow Sleeves

Princess Ilse, The Giant's Daughter

YOUNG ADULT NOVELS

Young Adult Fantasy (with elements of romance)

Elf Sight

Earth Bound

Young Adult Urban Fantasy

Stone Warrior (with elements of romance)

The Jungle Inside

Young Adult Contemporary (with elements of romance)

Through Your Eyes

The Ugly Stepsister

Perfect Little Princess

Young Adult Contemporary/Paranormal

Whispers In The Dark (with elements of romance and same sex relationships)

Over Too Soon (with elements of romance)

Young Adult Sci-Fi

Experiment X-One-Six (Urban Sci-Fi/Superheroes)

An Endless Dawn (Post Apocalyptic Sci-Fi)

CHILDREN'S BOOKS

Dragon Lord (Preteen/early teens) (Fantasy)

The Irish Wizard (Upper middle grade) (Urban Fantasy)

SHORT STORIES

Urban Fantasy

Eternally Late

Dealings With Joe

Glimpses (short story in That Moment When Anthology)

Contemporary

The Brat Next Door

Fantasy LitRPG

(Set in the same world as Guardians Of The Round Table Series)

Tales Of Inadon 1: The Disc (Co-written with Storm and Rhys Petersen) (short story in Game On! Anthology)

Post Apocalyptic Sci-Fi

Compulsive Directive

NONFICTION

A Year Of Weekly Writing Exercises (Creative Writing)

Cooking For Families With Allergies (Cooking) (Co-written with Storm Petersen)

Tell Me A Story, Grandma (Memoir)

For the most up to date details on available titles visit:

www.avrilsabine.com/books/bibliography

Dragon Blood Series

To learn more about this series visit:

www.avrilsabine.com/series/db

BOOKS AVAILABLE IN THE DRAGON BLOOD SERIES

(5 book series)

Book 1: Pliethin

Book 2: Wyvern

Book 3: Surety

Book 4: Knight

Book 5: Mage

BOOKS SET IN THE SAME WORLD AS THE DRAGON BLOOD SERIES

Dragon Mage- Young Adult Urban Fantasy (with elements of romance)

(Series two of Dragon Blood series)

Book 1: Promise

Dragon Blood Chronicles- Young Adult Urban Fantasy (with elements of romance)

(Companion stand alone series to Dragon Blood)

Book 1: Oath

Book 2: Betrayed

Disclaimer

This is a work of fiction. Names, characters, businesses, places, events and incidents are either the products of the author's imagination or used in a fictitious manner. Any resemblance to actual persons, living or dead, or actual events is purely coincidental. The opinions expressed or beliefs held are those of the characters and should not be assumed to be the opinions or beliefs of the author.